Claudia Quash
Book 1
The Spell of Pencliff

Wendy Hobbs

Onion Custard Publishing Ltd

Claudia Quash Series
Book 1: The Spell of Pencliff

© 2015 Wendy Hobbs
Cover illustration & Claudia Quash emblem © 2015 Annie Giles Hobbs

British Library Cataloguing in Publication Data.
A catalogue record for this book is available from the British Library.

Published in the United Kingdom by
Onion Custard Publishing Ltd, UK.
www.onioncustard.com
Twitter @onioncustard
Facebook.com/OnionCustardPublishing

Paperback format: ISBN: 978-1-909129-71-9

First Edition: October, 2015
Category: Teenage Mystery & Magic

I dedicate this book to
Jean and Terry Fordham,
my loving parents.

And to my beautiful, adventurous daughter,
Claudia, who inspired this story.

CONTENTS

1

A LETTER FROM BEYOND THE GRAVE

Claudia ran to the front door, bursting with happiness and yanked it open. She was expecting a special parcel for her birthday but found herself staring at a faceless stranger surrounded by a thick fog. He stepped forward, grabbed her wrist, squeezed it tightly, and shouted something harsh.

His voice drained the blood from her face and her heart beat wildly in her chest. She screamed and tried to pull away, but he was too strong, so she kicked him hard in the shin, again and again. He recoiled and his grip loosened just enough for her to break free. Then he disappeared into the misty street. She staggered back shakily, falling heavily against the grandfather clock behind her, gasping and dazed. The clock chimed loudly in her ear.

Claudia shot up in her bed to the sound of the clock striking the hour. She took a deep shuddering breath, and wiped perspiration from her brow. The struggle with a stranger, and the uncontrollable fear it had created within her, had seemed so real. Her hands were shaking. She shook her head, frowning thoughtfully. *Just a dream… just a bad dream. It doesn't mean anything.* As she slid out of bed, the nightmare dissipated. Her mood lifted when she spotted the calendar on the wall.

'At last, the sixteenth of December. I'm thirteen!'

She exploded with excitement and spun around on her tiptoes. 'Finally, I'm a teenager – old enough to do stuff without my parents tagging along.' She suddenly stopped and slumped back on her bed. 'But who with?' It occurred to her then that all her friends were away for the holidays. She didn't even have any brothers or sisters to hang around with.

Claudia pulled back the curtains to let in the sunlight and gasped. An enormous pile of snow lay on the lawn. *I wonder where this came from.* She'd never seen snow like it before in Pettifog. And what were those strange-looking birds? The garden was covered in bouncing black and white birds with bright orange beaks.

The door burst open. 'Happy birthday!' exploded a cheerful voice. Claudia beamed at her mother who rushed into the room. She flung her arms around her daughter and Claudia felt a great, big sloppy kiss land on her cheek.

'Mum,' complained Claudia, breaking free. 'I'm not a baby anymore.'

'Do you feel any older?' asked her mother, her blue eyes sparkling in her pale face.

Claudia thought for a moment. She'd felt pretty grown-up before today, but now she was thirteen she was looking forward to making her own decisions, following her heart, and having more freedom.

'You can tell me at breakfast!' Mum giggled and handed Claudia a bunch of envelopes. 'Why don't you open your cards while I get it ready.'

'Thank you.' Claudia gave a small smile but inside she sighed. She remembered how dull birthdays could be in the Christmas holidays. Having breakfast wasn't exactly exciting.

'I won't be long,' her mother said, closing the door behind her gently as she left the bedroom.

Claudia collapsed into her purple flower-print

armchair, and tucked her legs under her to study the pile of post on her lap. Most of it was the usual birthday mail – white envelopes from distant family she barely knew.

But one was different. She was drawn to an envelope with black spidery handwriting. There was something unfamiliar about it, like it didn't belong with the others. She held it up to the light. *This doesn't look like a birthday card!* She ripped it open and quickly unfolded the contents. Inside, there was a letter and an old, tattered, black and white photograph of two small people holding hands. It was marked on the back *Jasper* and *Daisy*. Daisy was wearing a high-collared dress and Jasper was in a very old-fashioned three-piece suit. She read the letter.

Dear Claudia,

I write to you from a prison cell. I am your great-grandfather and I was married to Daisy, your great-grand mother. We always dreamed of meeting you, but it wasn't meant to be. Tragically, Daisy was hung for a crime that she did not commit and her body is still buried within the prison walls in Pencliff. Once I was released, I fought hard for a pardon for her, even after her death, but I never managed to change the past. Sadly, I was disowned by the family and forced to move away, to hide my shame and start a new life. As you are our only grandchild, I dearly hope that you have the courage to continue the fight.

Please don't mention any of this to your parents, as I am sure they wouldn't want you to get involved.

You will find something that will help you at 6, Littleton Place, London.

Much love, Jasper Ratchet

Is this some kind of joke? If it was a joke, it wasn't a very funny one. She inspected the photograph more closely. It looked real. Maybe they really were her great-grandparents.

Claudia's heart missed a beat and tears welled in her eyes. Her mum and dad had never mentioned Jasper and Daisy. Had they really disowned them? Surely nobody would do something like that? It seemed so unfair. She picked up the picture and traced her fingers across their faces.

'I'd love to have met you both,' she said, wishing that some magical force could whisk her back in time so she could meet them. *Why didn't anyone tell me?*

Claudia held up the letter and noticed something stuck to the bottom. She lifted it up, realising it was a newspaper cutting that had yellowed with age.

The Pencliff News, 5th April 1900
JEWEL THIEF CAUGHT
The police are holding a suspect in custody who is believed to have murdered an innocent housekeeper for a rare diamond. A reward is being offered to anyone with information that could lead to a conviction being made…

She skim-read the rest of the article. *So it is real!* Her eyes widened. That was all the proof she needed. Nobody she knew could fake an old newspaper.

This must have been the crime that was linked to Daisy. *But what can I do about it now? It was so long ago.* She knew this was just the kind of adventure she was looking for. It was totally a thirteen-year-old thing to do. Despite her sadness for Daisy's death, she couldn't help but experience a surge of excitement.

'Breakfast!' called her mother from the kitchen.

Claudia hid the letter under her mattress and stomped downstairs. She had no idea what she would do about it, but she decided to keep it a secret for now, just as Jasper had wanted.

2

PUFFIN POST

When she entered the dining room, her mother was sitting with a plate piled high with banana pancakes – Claudia's favourite. She was listening to the radio.

'*A most mysterious migration is happening, right here in Pettifog. A leading ornithologist has reported that flocks of puffins are circling the town. Postal workers have complained that they are pinching their letters and delivering them to the right house, in half the time.*' The newsreader stifled a laugh. '*And now, over to Bill Slattery, weather service spokesman. Where's all this bad weather coming from, Bill?*'

'*It's a meteorological nightmare, Ron. While we're blanketed in six inches of snow, the rest of the country is set for the warmest Christmas ever, and basking in glorious sunshine. Listeners and expert meteorologists have reported that a giant snow cloud has got stuck above the town and refuses to budge.*'

'*That's Pettifog for you!*' said Ron.

Claudia's mother turned down the radio.

'I saw puffins outside the gates this morning, sat on our letterbox at the end of the path. Maybe *they* delivered your birthday cards.'

A letter from beyond the grave! Heavy snow! Puffins flying about all over the place! What on earth is happening?

'Is something bothering you, Claudia?' Her

mother studied her puzzled expression. 'I've made your favourite... banana pancakes.'

'Oh... nothing.' Claudia shook her head, her black wavy hair bouncing around, and took a seat. She was determined to keep her secret under wraps, but even the delicious sweet pancake smell couldn't take her mind off Daisy and Jasper. Could it be true?

'I know that you get lonely here all by yourself,' her mother said, leaning over the pancakes towards Claudia. 'Let's do something special for your birthday. We don't have to stay at home all day!'

An idea popped into Claudia's head right away. 'Could we visit Littleton Place, in London?' she pleaded. She knew it was a long trip but she had to start investigating immediately.

Her mother's forehead creased in a frown. 'Why do you want to go there? I'd thought maybe the zoo, or the theme park, would be fun.'

On any other day, those things might have excited Claudia, but not today. 'Umm... I've heard it has some amazing shops.' She made up the fib on the spot, hoping this would be enough to persuade her mother, who loved to go shopping.

'Well if that's what you'd like to do most of all, it's alright with me. But we'll have to wait until your father's home.' Her father was a lawyer and travelled a lot, which meant he often stayed away from home.

'When will he be back?' Claudia asked, pulling the top pancake from the stack, her appetite returning now that she was getting somewhere.

'Any minute now.' Claudia's mother got up from the table. 'I'll go and check the train times.'

Claudia swung round, mid-bite. Through the sash windows she could see her father straightening his silk tie as the automatic wrought iron gates sluggishly pushed open, forcing aside freshly fallen snow. He hurried down the drive, and Claudia noticed something tucked under his arm. Her birthday present? She rushed out into the hallway, wrapping her dressing gown around her tightly as the door opened and a blast of icy air shot in.

'What's that you're carrying?' asked her mother, raising an eyebrow at her husband.

'Is it a present for me?' Claudia knew it was rude to ask, but she couldn't help it. Her dad always got her interesting gifts. Last year he bought her a box of indoor fireworks and a pair of ice skates.

His lined face flashed beetroot. 'Not really,' he admitted. 'I'm afraid I've been rather busy…'

He let his arm drop and something black and furry jumped out. Claudia gasped and gulped… and gasped again. Staring back at her from the floor were two enormous pink eyes, sparkling brighter than a thousand-carat diamond.

'Wow, I don't believe it!' Claudia squealed. 'A cat? You got me a cat!'

The exotic black creature furiously slashed his tail from side to side, seeming just as excited to see Claudia, as she was to see him.

'He's so unusual.' Claudia crouched down and lovingly gathered the cat into her arms. He snuggled into her warmth and purred. She sank her hands into a deep pile of silky soft fur and stroked the white crescent-moon patch on his head.

'I found him wandering around outside,' her father said. 'I've never seen him around here before. I think he must be a stray. When I bent down to see if he had a collar, he leapt right into my arms!'

Claudia tore her eyes away from the cat to look at her mother. 'I *can* keep him, can't I?'

Her mum's look was one of disapproval. 'Pets are a lot of work and make a mess, Claudia. What happens when you're back at school?'

Claudia's face fell; she'd never felt as desperate to

have a pet as she did at that moment. 'But *please*, Mum. Now I'm home from boarding school I always get so lonely in the holidays,' she pleaded, her dark eyes enormous in her porcelain face. 'Besides, cats are very independent. He won't need much looking after. I'll make sure I feed him every day.'

Claudia swivelled round to face her father.

'I absolutely love him. Please?'

'I suppose there's no harm,' he said, gently nudging his wife. 'We can see how he gets on for a few days, at least. And he did seem to know exactly where I was taking him.'

The edges of her mother's mouth curled up the tiniest amount, and hope sprang in Claudia's heart.

'Well, he does look an awful lot like you – the same piercing eyes, silky black hair, and graceful long legs – like a ballerina.' Her mother nodded her head and said, 'I suppose it would be nice for you to have some company for a change.'

Claudia beamed so hard her face ached. 'Thank you! Thank you! Thank you!'

'What will you call him?' her mother asked.

Claudia looked into her cat's intense pink eyes and the name popped into her head. 'Sekora Black.'

'I like it!' her father said with a grin, 'How on earth did you think of that?'

'I'm not sure,' Claudia shook her head. 'But I know that it has to be something special.'

'You'd better put the cat in your bedroom if we're off to London,' suggested her mother.

Her father raised an eyebrow. 'Why London?'

'My birthday treat.' Claudia skipped up the stairs to her bedroom, her cat tucked safely under her arm. She felt a surge of excitement at the prospect of a new adventure. She had to find out more about her family and Jasper. *Things were looking up!*

3

AN UNUSUAL STORM

When Claudia returned to her bedroom she laid Sekora down gently on her bed and sat beside him. Whispering to him gently, she stroked his head and admired his beautiful, bright eyes.

'You're the best present I've ever had – even if you weren't meant to be one.'

Claudia jumped up and dragged open the wardrobe. 'I'd better get going.' She pulled out a warm woolly jumper, jeans, and a purple coat with a fur collar. She got dressed quickly, grabbed a book to read on the train, and took her purse off her dressing table. She dropped them into her favourite striped canvas tote bag. She turned back to Sekora and frowned when she realised his eyes had become dull and lifeless.

'Make yourself at home.' Claudia leant forward, tickled Sekora's ear, and said, 'I'll try not to be too long in London.'

Sekora meowed, showing his sharp teeth and looking at her bag. It was obvious to Claudia what he wanted.

'I'm not sure cats are allowed on trains.' Claudia was starting to think that he understood every word she said. 'Even if they were, my parents would never let me bring you.'

In one smooth move, Sekora jumped off the bed and wrapped his long black tail around Claudia's leg.

She tried to break free, but his grip only tightened. She couldn't shake him off. His tail was exceptionally strong for a cat. It seemed that Sekora wanted to come to London too.

'You win,' blurted out Claudia, all the time worrying how much trouble she'd be in with her parents. 'But you'd better behave.'

A loud horn sounded three times in quick succession. The large black gates slowly swung open and a car made its way carefully down the snowy drive.

'Hurry up!' her mother shouted up the stairs. 'The taxi is here.'

'Don't make a sound, Sekora.' Claudia lifted out the book from her bag and gently replaced it with the cat. With the bag over one shoulder, she stepped carefully down the winding staircase, across the hallway, and rushed outside to the taxi.

'Got everything you need?' asked her father.

Claudia took a deep breath and nervously nodded. She got into the car and gently placed the bag on her lap. She wondered whether she should just tell her parents that she had Sekora, but decided that it wasn't a good idea. Not when they were close to home. Instead, she focussed on Littleton Place, hoping desperately that she'd find out more about her mysterious relatives. Perhaps, if she was lucky, she could help to clear Daisy's name. She hoped it did have shops, as she'd told her mother. Otherwise she would get suspicious.

Her mother said, staring out of the taxi window, 'The weather's getting worse. According to this morning's newspaper, the snow is spreading to London. Perhaps it was a bad idea to travel today.'

'Stop worrying,' insisted Claudia. 'We'll be at the station before we know it.'

The taxi crawled to the end of the road. It turned up Fish Street and under Castle Bridge towards a gravelly road that ran alongside the river, then joined the main road into the town.

Her father shook his head and groaned. 'Maybe we should turn back.'

'You can't change your mind now,' urged Claudia. 'It is my birthday.'

'I suppose you're right.' His face softened. 'Any idea what you're looking for in London?'

Claudia gulped nervously. 'I'm sure I'll find something interesting.'

The driver blasted the horn and waved his fist out of the window. 'Watch out!' he shouted, at children who were throwing snow balls at the car, splattering them against the windows.

Claudia barely noticed. She was thinking so hard about Jasper's letter. *I wonder if I'll find anything in London that'll help me to clear Daisy's name?*

'I hope Sekora will be alright,' her mother sighed. 'We should have left him some food.'

The warmth coming from the cat on Claudia's lap burned into her legs. She felt her face turning bright red.

When the taxi came to a halt outside Pettifog Station, Claudia held on tight to her bag. She opened the door and stepped onto the pavement. 'I'll get the tickets!' she said, desperate to prove to her parents that she was capable of looking after herself now that she was a teenager.

'Very well,' her father said, in his business-like manner, passing her some money. 'But be quick.'

Claudia entered the station. It was unusually busy for the time of day. Although, she reminded herself, it was the holidays, and people did like to travel to London to see the Christmas lights and shop displays. She looked up at the large clock. Both of its hands were approaching twelve. She rushed past a newsagent where a plump little man was waving copies of the morning paper. 'Extra! Extra! Read all about it. Thief murdered for a rare stolen jewel.'

Claudia stared at the headline on the newspaper: *Daisy Ratchet in Custody*. Her stomach flipped and she suddenly felt sick. She stopped, glanced at the newspaper again and focussed on the words. She was mistaken. It actually read: *Suspect in Custody*. She breathed a huge sigh of relief and pushed past people entering and leaving the concourse. A loud voice echoed in her ears, announcing arrival and departure times. She paused for a moment outside a bookshop, concentrating on the announcements. There was a train to London in fifteen minutes.

Claudia felt a cold hand grip her shoulder that jerked her senses back to the nightmare she'd woken from that morning of the faceless stranger. The hand caught her by surprise. Immediately a chill skittered down her spine, and she jumped, as if she'd been shot.

4

A MYSTERIOUS BOOK

'Stop dawdling,' mumbled her mother, rushing through the station, pulling Claudia's elbow along with her. 'We need to get the tickets!'

'You scared me,' blurted out Claudia, trying to keep up.

They quickened their pace, but soon came to an abrupt halt, surprised to see long, snake-like queues of people at every ticket booth. They forced themselves through a sea of bodies, until a guard directed them towards a booth just selling tickets to London. They joined the end of the queue and after several minutes, they shuffled forward towards a chubby face peering through the window of the booth. 'Three tickets to London please,' said Claudia, handing over the money.

'Certainly,' came the reply, 'but you'd better be quick. The train's leaving in less than five minutes.'

'There you are,' Claudia's father said as they found him back on the concourse. 'Let's get going.'

They hurried over to platform six, and less than a minute later a purple train appeared in the station. Sweet papers, used tickets, and torn-up pieces of a newspaper drifted in and out of the crowds of feet pressing towards the edge of the platform, everyone eager to grab an empty seat. Claudia was first to enter the train, towards a guard, huffing and puffing. He stepped forward, looking the passengers up and down.

'Tickets please.'

'Here.' Claudia smiled and held out all three.

'Thank you,' he said, punching the tickets before handing them back to her. 'Have a good journey.'

Claudia led the way to the back of the carriage, until she found an empty table with four seats. She carefully placed her bag on the seat nearest to the window and sat down in the aisle seat. So far Sekora hadn't made a sound, but this didn't stop her worrying that at any moment he might try to escape. Her mother and father took their seats opposite.

'What's this?' Claudia felt something poking up into her thigh. She pulled out a black shabby book stuffed down the side of the seat and lay it on the table. She read the title on the cover. *'The History of Pencliff,'* she said, then flicked through the pages, grumbling that it didn't contain any pictures, or even a map of the place.

'That's where my family are from,' Claudia's father mumbled, 'but I haven't been there for years.'

'Really?' replied Claudia, surprised 'Can you take me there after Christmas?' Her dad had never talked much about his family, and his parents had died before Claudia was born.

'We'll see,' her father said, shifting uncomfortably in his seat. 'None of my relatives are alive, so there seems little point, really.'

'What a coincidence,' said her mother, catching her husband's eye. 'That should be an interesting read for you.

'Mmm,' he said with disinterest. 'While you were getting the tickets, I picked up a newspaper and this month's edition of *The Lawyers' Journal.*' He handed it to his wife saying, 'I know you like to keep up to date with the latest criminal cases. There is an interesting murder trial reported on the second page that my colleague at work has been involved in.'

'Did you know the family?' she asked.

'I've heard of them,' he said, clearing his throat. 'They're a very well-off family that live in a large house by the coast.'

Her mum's blue eyes narrowed. 'So the killer was after something?'

'The usual,' he nodded. 'Jewellery, I guess, because it can easily be dismantled, reset and sold. But the police caught the killer with fingerprint evidence.'

'I miss the law so much, even if the job was stressful.' Her mother shook her head and sighed heavily. 'It gave me so much satisfaction when the right person was caught and convicted of the crime.'

Dad tilted his head at Claudia and said, 'Now that Claudia's getting older, I'm sure you'll be able to take on some part-time work.'

'You're probably right,' her mother smiled, and began skimming through the pages of the journal.

Claudia picked up the guidebook and settled back in her seat. She read about an ancient coastal town with two prominent hills, renowned for its peculiar weather patterns. On one hill stood Pencliff Castle and on the other was a gallows where criminals were once hung. In the centre of the town was a bronze statue of the first ruler, Ambrose Ashworth, sitting on a horse and surrounded by a courthouse, pastel-coloured townhouses, and small bow-fronted shops.

The book said that when Ambrose died, the town quickly descended into crisis and criminal activity soared, until they appointed Septimus Snail, a ruthless man who established a strict rule of law. During his reign, he became sole judge and jury in order to topple the corrupt powers that kept the town from prospering. He mercilessly sent convicted criminals to the gallows. Legend has said that a notorious thief, called Leakey Porridge, was hung for stealing, and still haunted Pencliff Castle. At his trial he cursed the ruler, saying that all his descendants would be born blind, deaf, and dumb. They say that his soul still walks the battlements, late at night, wailing and whining and tearing at the noose tied around his neck.

'How is your book?' asked her father.

'OK.'

Claudia's heart was sinking into her stomach. She thought that the town sounded like a really creepy place. She continued to read about how the relatively peaceful island changed after Ambrose died and became a target for cutthroats and pirates. They descended upon the town and subjected their victims to horrifying torture, smuggled cargo into the harbour, plotted dirty deals, and sold stolen goods.

An hour into the journey, heavy rain started to lash the train, blurring the view of the snowy countryside. As the train sped further south, black clouds appeared and a low rumbling sound filled the air. Claudia put the book down. She really wanted to carry on reading about Pencliff but she couldn't concentrate. She was far too busy worrying about Sekora.

'Meow! Meow!'

'What's that noise?' Her mother glanced around.

'Meow.' Claudia giggled nervously, her heart thumping in her chest. She pulled her bag towards her, trying to comfort Sekora. 'It's only me messing around.'

'You're a funny girl sometimes.' Her mother returned to her magazine and started scanning the section on job vacancies.

Claudia hugged her bag and stared out of the window at the incoming storm. A strong wind ruffled the trees as the sky darkened. The lights inside the carriage came on, then flickered and dimmed.

'Why is it so dark outside?' Claudia was worried that the weather was upsetting Sekora.

'It'll soon pass,' her father assured her without looking up from his newspaper.

Just then, the train swished through a long, dark tunnel and the carriage violently rocked from side to side. As it emerged at the other end, the sky lit up with lightning bolts and cracks of thunder that pierced Claudia's ears.

'Meow! Meow!'

Her mother dropped her magazine. 'Please... don't tell me that you've brought the cat! I should have known!'

Her father covered his face with his newspaper, unsuccessfully trying to hide a smirk.

'Please don't be angry.' Claudia knew there was no way they'd believe it was her making noises this time. She wasn't that good at animal impressions. 'Sekora wouldn't stay at home, honestly. He wrapped his tail around me and wouldn't let go!'

Her mother rolled her eyes. 'You'd better keep him quiet or the guard might throw us off the train.'

'There now, Sekora, I'll look after you.' Claudia gently reached into her bag and lovingly stroked his shaking body. As the thunder rumbled, Sekora whined, as if in terrible pain. He crawled out of the bag onto her lap and, seeing the book on the table, he meowed.

'It's only a book on Pencliff.'

As Claudia pulled it towards her, Sekora's paw flashed forward and he scratched the cover with his claws.

Claudia's mind was racing. She didn't know how it was possible, but she wondered if Sekora knew the town. Was there was a reason why he was reacting so strangely to the storm? Her head spun with questions for which she had no answers. But she was determined to find out!

5

SPLINTS

By the time they pulled into London, the dark sky had brightened. A polite voice echoed through the train: 'We will be arriving at Paddington Station in two minutes' time. Please remember to collect all of your belongings.'

Claudia gently returned Sekora to her bag. She stood, lifted the bag onto her shoulder, and joined the impatient passengers shuffling along the narrow aisle. As the train rumbled to a stop she followed her parents out of the door and onto the platform. Now they'd arrived, Claudia's stomach flipped nervously. *What if no-one has heard of Jasper in Littleton Place? What will I do next? I have to find some answers!*

'Stay close to us,' shouted her mother, a few heads away. 'It's easy to go missing in this crowd.' Claudia nodded, still lost in thoughts about Jasper and Daisy.

They headed down a flight of steep steps and joined a hurrying stream of people pouring onto the snowy pavement outside the station. They quickly made their way across the road to join the queue for the black taxi cabs. After shuffling forward every so often, they reached the front of the line.

'Can you take us to Littleton Place?' her father asked the taxi driver.

'Alright, mate,' he replied, 'been back and forth there all morning!'

'Why?' asked Claudia.

'Everyone flocks to Littleton Place at Christmas,' he laughed loudly. 'You'll love it.'

Wondering what he meant, Claudia opened the door and gently placed her bag on the floor. She didn't want the driver to know she was carrying a cat – she had no idea what the rule about pets in taxis was in London.

The driver swung the steering wheel and the car veered from side to side on the slushy road. The streets were bustling with traffic, and impatient drivers tooted their horns and shook their fists in frustration.

'As soon as it snows,' the driver said, 'people panic and the traffic completely shuts down the roads.'

'This is going to take forever.' Claudia was beginning to wonder if they'd ever get there.

'I'll take a short cut.' The driver made some quick turns, through back-streets, eventually squeezing the car along a winding alleyway flanked by thick trees that met overhead and created a gloomy tunnel. At the end of the alleyway he turned right and the car came to a standstill in a street lined with quaint little shops. Everything was decorated with twinkling trees and strings of shimmering snowflakes. Ahead, vehicles queued up for as far as Claudia could see.

Claudia thought back to the lie she told her mum, feeling relieved. *At least there are shops here, like I said.*

'Just here will do,' her mother said, spotting a designer dress shop with a pale blue evening gown in the window.

The driver stopped the car. 'That'll be nine-eighty please.'

'Can I look around on my own?' Claudia quickly opened the door and stepped out of the cab. She couldn't ask questions about Jasper with her parents hanging around. 'We could meet up again in an hour?'

'That's fine,' her mother nodded and smiled. 'I

know you're sensible, and you are thirteen now, after all!'

Holding her bag close to her, Claudia strode along the road, her gaze shifting from one side of the street to the other, looking for number six. She couldn't see many numbers on the shop signs, just their names. She crossed the road and hurried along, but was stopped by a large crowd of shoppers. She decided she'd have to ask for directions if she was ever going to find it before she had to meet her parents again.

'Excuse me,' Claudia said to a short, stout man in the crowd, 'I'm looking for six Littleton Place.'

'You and everyone else around here,' he said, pointing his finger at the shop window just down the road. Claudia followed it to the impressive bow-fronted shop, which she saw was called *Splints*. She edged past people towards the window, but it was in total darkness. Catching a stranger's eye, she asked, 'Has this always been a shop?'

'Err... I think so,' he replied, scratching his head.

'Have you heard of Jasper Ratchet?'

'I'm afraid not,' he replied, shaking his head, 'although, I haven't lived around here for long.'

Claudia gazed hopelessly at the crowd. She wondered if someone might have heard of Jasper. 'What's everyone waiting for?'

'The Christmas display will be unveiled any minute now,' he answered. 'I'd stay put if I were you.'

With her bag weighing heavily on her shoulder, Claudia carefully put it down. Sekora immediately jumped out and mewed with delight. Claudia grinned and tickled his ears. 'So, you want to have a look too.'

A pair of large, wrinkled hands appeared at the window, slowly dragging aside a heavy crimson curtain.

'Wow!' gasped the crowd in unison.

Claudia stared at the beautiful Georgian doll's

house that had been revealed. It was as tall as her, and almost the same in width. The grand hallway had a sweeping staircase, and the rooms were graced with glittering chandeliers and exquisite antique furniture. She peered into its tiny rooms, studying every detail. There were porcelain dolls in everyday poses – one standing next to a fireplace, others talking together, while some listened to musicians playing minuscule instruments.

'It's amazing,' she said to Sekora. She froze for several seconds, lost in the midst of its magic. 'I wish I could have this at home…' she paused 'Although, I guess I am a *bit* old for a doll's house.'

Sekora purred and pawed the window.

'*Splints*,' a man shouted loudly enough to be heard over the crowd, 'is the best place to bring the kids at Christmas.'

'Look at the toys!' squealed an excited little girl with bright red bows in her hair.

Claudia looked into the nursery, thinking that it must hold every toy imaginable. She could see balls, puzzles, bikes, dolls, clockwork trains whizzing around tracks, and enamel dogs with fierce faces. There was even a creepy castle with a dungeon where tiny tin soldiers were holding swords alongside scary skeletons in chains.

'It's so authentic,' said a woman in a frightfully posh voice, wearing a frightfully posh hat with a purple feather.

Claudia beamed as she let her imagination run wild. She pressed her nose against the icy cold window, studying the high-society ball that was taking place in the drawing room. The host wore a black tailcoat and the lady beside him was dressed in a beautiful purple silk gown encrusted with gemstones.

'Look at that cute cat in the hall,' a boy beside Claudia shouted.

Stroking Sekora's back, Claudia said, 'He reminds me of you!' Sekora let out a strange squealing sound. *Can he really understand exactly what I'm saying?*

As time ticked by, Claudia imagined herself inside the doll's house, mounting the wide stone steps towards the front door. The sound of the bell rang in her ears. In her mind she hurried into the hall and started playing hide and seek with Sekora, who was hiding first. She raced around the place, searching every cubbyhole and corner, and then she rushed up the staircase, but she couldn't find him. As she dashed into a bedroom, the vision faded and she remembered that she wasn't really in the house, but outside the shop window, looking in.

'Come on, Sekora,' Claudia said, gathering him up and dropped him carefully into her bag. He didn't seem to mind. 'If we are ever going to find out what all of this mystery around Daisy and Jasper is about, we're going to have to go inside.'

6

A JOURNEY IN TIME

A bell tinkled as sweetly as a sleigh bell, as Claudia pushed open the door. She crept inside the empty shop. The crowd were still outside admiring the window display. It was a large, old-fashioned shop with rickety floorboards and shelves from floor to ceiling, jam-packed with models that perfectly replicated the real thing. Tiny chairs for tiny tables, dozens of dolls with glass eyes, horses and carriages, and pieces of diamond jewellery that were so small they resembled glitter.

'Good afternoon.'

Claudia spun around so fast she nearly lost her footing.

An old man wearing a red velvet waistcoat and a gold watch chain stood behind a counter that ran the length of one wall.

'I'm Sydney Splint,' he said, peering over his half-moon glasses. 'What can I do for you?'

'Hello, I'm Claudia Quash,' she said wondering what to say next. As she shuffled towards him she could see herself reflected in his little glasses. She placed her bag on the floor, sucked in a deep breath and said, 'I came in to congratulate you on building such an amazing doll's house.'

Sydney raised his eyebrows and said, 'Thank you very much, but I have to admit that I never made it. I found it in the workshop when I took over the old place many years ago, and I decided that this year I'd spruce it up and use it for the Christmas display.'

'Did you know whose it was?' asked Claudia, her hopes rising.

'Well, yes, it belonged to the old watchmaker who owned the shop before me,' Sydney nodded. 'Mr Ratchet... I forget his first name.'

'Jasper!' blurted Claudia. When Sydney frowned, she explained: 'He was my great-grandfather.' Claudia wasn't sure whether she should have admitted this, but it was too late to take it back.

'I see,' said Sydney. 'Sadly I never met him.'

'Do you know what happened to him?'

'I heard that he had to shut the shop.'

'Why was that?'

'Err... his wife was in some sort of trouble with the police.'

Claudia's eyes widened. Now, she was convinced that the letter was real and her great-grandmother had been hung for murder. *It was all true.*

'Since you're a relative, let me show you this.' Sydney turned around, opened up the back of the doll's house and placed a tiny grandfather clock on the counter. 'I found it inside the doll's house, next to the clockwork cat, but it doesn't work. It seems strange considering that was his job. It's a shame; I won't feel like the house is complete until I can get it working.'

So that's it. Jasper built the doll's house. Claudia felt like she was getting a bit closer to solving the mystery. As she picked up the clock, her fingers felt warm and her heart beat faster. It was a very unusual clock. On the face were two planets set either side of a seascape. As one moon disappeared behind a planet on the right side, another popped up on the left side. And instead of numbers, twelve little moons illuminated a strange inscription. '*A Journey in Time*,' said Claudia. 'I wonder what Jasper meant by that?'

'No idea,' replied Sydney. 'I took it to a horologist, who told me that it was a moon dial that tells the time in accordance with its phases. Unfortunately, he couldn't fix it. He tried a number of different springs but they weren't small enough, and he even made one especially for the clock, but it still wouldn't work.'

'Maybe Jasper died before he had time to finish it.' Claudia pondered, as she put it down.

'Maybe. I've tried everything,' Sydney sighed heavily.

'Can I buy it?' Claudia didn't know why, but she thought it might somehow give her an insight into Jasper's world.

'I'm sorry,' said Sydney, shaking his head, 'but I never sell anything that doesn't work. I can't risk the complaints, you see.'

Claudia's face fell. 'What about the doll's house?' She was desperate to have something of Jasper's. 'Is that for sale?'

'I'd never sell the doll's house.' Sydney took the clock from the counter and returned it to its rightful place.

'Are you sure?' said Claudia, her throat tight with disappointment.

'Have a look around.' Sydney gestured to the jam-packed shelves. 'I'm certain that something else will catch your eye.'

At that moment the door blew open, and Sekora yowled from inside the bag. Claudia quickly picked the bag up and hurried to one side. A couple entered the shop with a young girl, who rushed towards the counter waving a piece of paper in the air.

Sydney smiled kindly. 'What can I do for you?'

'Please can I have everything on this list?'

Claudia felt Sekora's tail lashing back and forth through the bag. She slipped behind a display cabinet, feeling panicky. She didn't want to leave, but she guessed Sydney would chuck her out of his shop if he found her with a cat. Sekora squirmed.

Claudia shuffled further behind the cabinet. At first she thought it was a dead end, until she saw a door handle in the wall. Without thinking, she twisted it and the door opened into a dark and dusty room. She rushed in, shut the door behind her and put down the bag. Sekora immediately leapt out and meowed grumpily, as if he'd had had enough of being confined.

Claudia looked in amazement at the walls. They were covered in clocks of all shapes and sizes, ticking away. 'This must have been Jasper's workshop. I guess they still haven't got rid of some of his old stuff,' she mumbled, heading towards a wooden workbench. She rummaged through broken clock cases, old pendulum bobs, and a selection of rusty springs. Her heart sank. *There's nothing here that can help me to clear Daisy's name.* Claudia picked up a broken clock with a loose spring and studied it for a few moments. As she scanned the room, she fiddled with the mechanism, stretching a spring and fixing it to the case of the clock. Then she absentmindedly grabbed a weight from the bottom of the case, attached it to the chain, and wound it around the ratchet wheel. Finally, she adjusted the pendulum rod, allowing it to swing from side to side, and the clock immediately started ticking.

'Good as new,' she said, then put the fixed clock on the bench and watched the second hand sweep around the dial. She had always had a knack for fixing things, and it helped her to work with things when she wanted to think. *I've brought you back to life!*

Claudia suddenly heard heavy footsteps. Sekora jumped at the noise, scampering across the wooden floor and squeezing himself through a gap in the skirting board.

'Come back, Sekora!' Claudia ran towards the

hole. 'You'll get lost.'

Then she heard a rattling sound and quickly spun around. The door slowly creaked open. Her body trembled and her pulse raced.

I shouldn't be here! She darted towards a hollow long-case clock, opened it, and hid inside, pulling the door shut just as someone entered the room. She held her breath and strained her ears to listen. *I hope I don't get found out!*

7

THE CLOCKWORK CAT

Claudia put an eye to the crack where the door hadn't quite shut. She saw Sydney standing beside the workbench, scratching his head and glancing around the room. 'Now where did I put that screwdriver?'

Claudia remained perfectly still as Sydney shuffled towards a shabby cupboard, opened it, and fumbled inside for a moment. 'Ahh… there it is!' He grabbed the missing tool and went back through the door, muttering to himself.

As soon as he'd left, Claudia bounded out from inside the clock. 'Sekora! Sekora!' she said, frantically pressing her ear against the wall where he'd disappeared, listening for any sign of him. She couldn't hear anything, so she started thumping the wall with her fist until it ached. 'Where are you?'

She was sure that the cat was trapped inside the wall. How would she get him out? When it seemed clear he wasn't coming back, Claudia slumped onto a spindly chair, furious at herself for bringing Sekora to London.

'I'm so stupid,' she told herself, shaking her head. It was then that she spotted the time on the clocks on the wall. She was late! She had to get back to her parents! Reluctantly, she staggered to her feet, took a deep breath, and tiptoed through the door.

She spotted her parents in the crowd of customers

now filling the shop. She came up beside her father, tugging on his arm.

'There you are,' he said, his frown fading into a smile. 'We thought you might have got distracted in here.' The creases in his forehead returned when he saw Claudia's face. 'What on earth is the matter?'

'I've lost Sekora,' spluttered Claudia. 'He's disappeared and I don't know where he's gone.'

'Never mind,' her mother hugged Claudia as if she'd lost a trinket, not her brand new pet, 'maybe he was meant to remain a stray.'

'Why don't you choose something nice for your birthday from here?' her father suggested.

'No,' Claudia shook her head, angry that her parents had no idea how upset she was. All she really wanted was Sekora to come back and she couldn't understand why he would run away. It was almost too much to bear on top of everything else she had to worry about.

'We can always buy another cat,' her father said softly. 'I'll ring the local pet shop in the morning.'

'Don't bother,' sniffed Claudia. 'There will never be another Sekora.' She knew how rude she sounded, but she couldn't help it. She squeezed past a group of children and made her way towards the counter. Sydney had heard the conversation and shot her a glum smile as she approached.

'Sydney, please can I buy the clockwork cat in the doll's house?' she asked. It wouldn't be the same, but at least the toy looked like Sekora.

'Sorry, but it's not for sale. The cat's a part of the doll's house. I've split things before and I always regret it.' Sydney pointed his finger at a glass cabinet full of cats. 'Why don't you choose one of those?'

Claudia's face dropped. 'But I really want that one.'

The front door opened, sending a flurry of snow

29

through the shop. Sydney looked up at the harassed people stomping in, pushing and shoving each other out of the way.

'I'd like to buy the Ideal Doll's House Starter Kit,' barked a big, beefy man with a beer belly. 'You'll need to be quick or I'll miss my bus.'

'I'm here to collect Mrs Clutterbuck's Christmas order, for the twenty-first of December,' snapped a severe-looking woman in a high-pitched voice. 'She rang yesterday and you promised that it would be ready by now.'

Claudia stood firm at the counter, pleading with her eyes at Sydney.

'Umm... umm... well as you're a relative of Jasper's,' sighed Sydney, adjusting his glasses. He swiftly grabbed the cat from the hallway of the doll's house, and placed it on the counter.

Claudia's pulse raced.

'Is that all you want?' exclaimed her mother, who was laden down with shopping bags which Claudia guessed were full of designer dresses. 'It's so small.'

'Is there anything else?' her father glanced round the shop. 'It is your birthday after all.'

'No,' Claudia said firmly. 'This is all I want.' If she couldn't have the clock, then this would be second best.

Sydney pulled open a drawer and picked out a small red gift box. He dropped the cat inside and handed it to Claudia. 'That'll be five pounds please.'

'I'll pay.' Her mother opened her purse and handed over the money.

Claudia lifted the lid and admired the clockwork cat. She felt sad about Sekora, but at least she had a present that looked just like him.

Her father cleared a path to the front door. 'We'd better get going or we'll miss our train.'

Claudia's heart sank and she shrugged off his

words. 'Maybe I should have one last look around for Sekora.'

'I'm sorry, it's getting late,' her mother gently nudged her elbow. 'We have to go.'

Claudia shook her head in puzzlement. She didn't want to go without finding him, but she knew her parents wouldn't wait. There was no other option. She had to leave her cat behind.

8

LOST AND FOUND

When they boarded the train Claudia was still upset about Sekora. Even though she'd only had him for a matter of hours, she'd felt an instant connection and was sad that she would never see him again. She collapsed into the seat next to the window and her parents sat opposite her.

'Can I get you anything, darling?' her father asked.

'No thanks.'

'You're not still upset about Sekora, are you?'

Claudia nodded her head and said, 'We were getting along so well together.'

'Try not to think about it.'

'I wish I'd left him at home.'

'Don't torture yourself.'

As the train trundled along, hitting bends and rocking from side to side like a cradle, Claudia sank back in her seat and sighed heavily. Her day had been a disaster. She felt sad about losing Sekora and she hadn't found any clues in *Splints*. *What will I do about the letter? Suppose I never solve the crime? Daisy is doomed!* Claudia felt drained of energy. Her mind spun over the same unanswerable questions, and she fell into an uneasy sleep.

She was hurrying along a dark winding road, lit by gas lights, going on and on, knowing that some dreadful place was at the end of it.

Time shifted and she stopped outside a prison. It was surrounded by large loops of razor wire on top of limestone walls. She rang a bell and after a while a toothless old guard ambled up, grunting and groaning deep in his chest. He unlocked the gates. Claudia dashed past him, and ran into a garden. She glanced around, spotting a weedy, overgrown grave with a cracked tree stump.

As Claudia moved closer, she felt a fire burning inside her. There was a blinding flash of lilac light. A spirit rose out of the grave and grabbed her hand. The ghost screamed and begged to be removed from its terrible place. As she yelped for someone to help her, Claudia spotted Daisy's name carved on the stump of wood.

Claudia woke with a start, shivering and shaking all over.

'You look like you've seen a ghost,' her father studied Claudia's face intently.

Claudia trembled as she said, 'I… I had a bad dream.' She realised why Jasper had never given up hope of getting a pardon for Daisy and how awful it must have been for him that she had been laid to rot in a dingy grave inside the prison. *I can't leave her there!*

Later that evening, Claudia hauled herself onto her bed. She missed Sekora terribly. And then there was her visit to *Splints*, which had been one big disappointment. *What do I do now? Perhaps I could tell Dad and he would be able to arrange a pardon for Daisy? I used to tell my parent's everything, but Jasper's letter clearly said that I shouldn't. This is a nightmare! I don't want to break Jasper's trust.*

Claudia took out the little red gift box from her pocket. She threw the lid to one side and stared into the black cat's pink eyes. She still couldn't believe that she had lost Sekora after less than a day. 'I wonder where he went?' she said to herself. 'Maybe my parents were right; maybe he was meant to be a stray.' That didn't make her feel any better, but at least she had the clockwork toy as a reminder.

'Claudia!' her mother shouted up the stairs. 'Come down and have something to eat.'

'I'll be there in a minute.'

Claudia dropped the cat back into the box and closed the lid. She sauntered down the stairs, and into the dining room. Her father was lighting the candelabra while her mother carried a large tray, laden with sandwiches, scones with raspberry jam, trifle, and a pink birthday cake.

'This looks delicious, darling,' said her father, lifting the plates of food onto the table. 'A proper birthday feast!'

Claudia slumped into the chair. 'I'm not that hungry.' She struggled to crack a smile, although she knew she should be grateful.

'You never refuse my homemade cake,' said her mother, sinking the knife into the thick pink icing, pulling out a slice, and handing it to Claudia on a plate. Claudia took the plate, broke off a tiny bit of cake, and nibbled at it. The sweet sponge tasted bitter to her.

'Eat up – there's plenty more where that came from,' said her father. 'Are you still upset about that cat?'

'I'm alright,' Claudia sighed, as she took another nibble.

That's good,' her father grinned. 'I wouldn't like it to spoil your birthday.'

Claudia noticed something, as she took in her father's smile. He looked exactly like Jasper in the photograph. He had the same shape eyes and even his nose had a prominent bridge just like her great-grandfather's. Her eyes flitted around the room. She hadn't really thought about it until now, but there weren't any family photographs in the house. All her grandparents had died before she was born, and they always spent Christmas alone.

Her father saw Claudia's sad expression and asked, 'What's wrong?'

'She's just tired,' said her mother, as she munched on a scone.

Claudia's throat tightened and she found herself choking on a lump of icing.

'Drink this.' Her mother handed her a glass of water. 'I think you should have an early night.'

Claudia took a big gulp. 'You're right. I think I'm going to go to bed.' She pushed her chair away from the table, thinking about the book and wondering whether it hadn't just been accidently left on the train. *Maybe it was to do with Jasper's letter. But how?*

'Goodnight, Claudia,' said her father as he helped himself to another sandwich. 'Sweet dreams.'

Claudia climbed the stairs, heading towards her room, but suddenly stopped. *Was that a noise coming from my room?* It had sounded like movement and made the hairs on the back of her neck bristle. Maybe she was imagining she heard something, or maybe not. Either way, she edged closer, pressing her ear to the wooden door, listening to a curious vibrating sound.

She squeezed the doorknob. It felt cold, sending an icy shiver through her veins, as if her body was being frozen and all sensation was about to vanish. Her hand turned. The door clicked open. She breathed fast and hard and her heart was pounding. Peeking inside, she gasped.

9

THE GOLDEN SPRING

'Sekora! How did you find your way home?' Claudia
blinked in disbelief.

Sekora purred loudly in reply from where he lay
curled up on a chair.

'I'm so happy you came back.' Claudia ran over
and stroked the white crescent-moon mark on his
head, which felt like the softest velvet. 'I thought I'd
never see you again.'

Sekora tilted his head to one side and winked.

'Now I've got two of you!'

Claudia sat on her bed, picked up the red box, and
looked inside. She frowned. The clockwork cat had
disappeared! She scrambled under the bed, rummaging
through old shoes and games, but it was nowhere. She
was sure she'd put it back safely in the box. She stood
up, checked the box once more, removing the tissue
paper, but it was gone.

'That's strange,' gasped Claudia. 'I'm sure I put it
back.'

Sekora jumped off the chair, onto the bed and
nestled beside her.

'But I'd rather have the real thing,' she smiled,
running her fingers through his warm fur. He rolled
over, as if he wanted to play. She tickled his tummy
and he licked her hand.

'What's that?' Claudia said, untangling a small

object that was stuck in his fur. It was a gold spring. She held it up and twisted it through her fingers. 'Where did you get this?'

Sekora yowled.

'I'm sure we'll find a use for it,' Claudia put the spring on her bedside table, switched off the lamp, and climbed into bed, yawning like a lion. Sekora leapt in beside her and snuggled up close. Claudia drifted off to sleep.

Claudia stepped inside Splints, *pushing past the people in the shop who were carrying heavy boxes. Glancing around, she searched for Jasper, desperate to tell him something. He wasn't there, so she hurried towards the back of the shop, feeling flustered. She flew through the door to the workshop.*

Jasper was sitting at his wooden bench, working away on his miniature grandfather clock. Claudia stood still for a moment, watching him. He was adding tiny chimes, cogs, wheels, a brass pendulum bob, and as he fitted the final spring, the silver hands on the moon dial spun backwards and the clock chimed loudly. Jasper's eyes lit up and he smiled. He looked up, spotting Claudia and tried to hand her the clock. He mumbled something but she couldn't hear what he said. She drew closer to him, her heart ticking in time with the clock, but before she could take it, someone fiercely grabbed her from behind. They dragged her backwards, preventing her from taking it.

A harsh voice rasped in her ear, 'Do you want to join Daisy on the gallows?' Claudia struggled hard to free herself, desperate to speak to Jasper and grab the clock, but the stranger tightened his grip and laughed loudly and coldly into her ear.

'Let me go!' she shouted, sitting bolt upright and breaking into a cold sweat. She sat there for a while in silence, shaking, and trying to calm herself down.

What a crazy dream that was!

As Claudia switched on her bedside lamp, the tiny

spring glistened, and glowed like a thread of coiled gold. She gazed at it for several seconds, reflecting on her dream. She remembered Jasper sat at his workbench, building his clock. When he had fitted the final spring, it had sprung to life. Maybe Jasper lost the spring, then died before he had chance to find it!

Claudia fixed her eyes on Sekora. 'Where did you find this spring, you clever cat?'

Sekora's pink eyes flashed like torches. Claudia sprinted out of her room, flew down the stairs, and skidded into the kitchen where her parents were sat at the kitchen table, drinking coffee.

'What's going on?' said her father, almost dropping his cup. 'I thought you'd be asleep by now.'

'I was, but I had a terrible nightmare.'

'Would you like a hot drink?'

'No thanks,' Claudia said quickly. 'We have to go back to London!'

But her mother wasn't paying attention. She was staring behind her instead. 'Look!' she interrupted 'Sekora's back.'

'Yeah, it's brilliant,' Claudia replied hastily, 'but can we go to London?'

'Where did he come from?' Her father scratched his head, not answering Claudia's question.

'He must have followed us home. I don't know. It's great! But I need to go and see Sydney.'

'What a clever cat,' her mother said, still ignoring her questions, much to Claudia's frustration.

'Why do you need to go to London?' Her father finally registered Claudia's demand and asked, 'What's so important there?'

'I think I've found the spring that will fix Sydney's grandfather clock.' Claudia couldn't tell them that it was actually Jasper's clock, and that she hoped it might somehow help her to clear Daisy's name.

'You're not making any sense,' said her father,

sipping his coffee. 'What clock are you talking about? Who's Sydney?'

'Sydney owns *Splints*. He showed me an amazing moon dial clock that was made for the doll's house,' said Claudia, trying to make it sound important. 'It doesn't work, even though he had a spring made especially for it.'

'We can't get back to London until the new year. I'm in court for the next few days and then it's Christmas.'

Claudia stepped nearer to her father and spoke softly. 'But what about the spring?'

'I'm sorry, darling. It'll have to wait.'

'We can go to London after Christmas,' her mother assured her, 'on New Year's Day, once the shops have reopened. I'd like to do some more clothes shopping.'

Her dad nodded and said, 'If the clock has never worked, a few more days won't make any difference.'

Mum put her hand on Claudia's shoulder. 'Now get some rest. You look exhausted.'

Claudia's breath came out in a groan. 'I suppose you're right.' She turned on her heels and stomped up to her room with Sekora scampering close beside her. She jumped onto her bed and stared up at the ceiling with her hands folded underneath her head. 'I don't want to wait until after Christmas. Sydney could fix the clock right now and maybe then he'd sell it to me with the doll's house.'

Sekora pounced onto the end of the bed and whined like a dog. Claudia sat up and stared at her cat, wishing that he could talk.

She switched off the bedside lamp and sank back into her soft pillow, sighing loudly. 'I've got to get back to London.' She had made up her mind and nothing would change it. *Even if it means going alone!'*

She snuggled down into her bed, yawned sleepily, and

burrowed deeper into her pillow. Her head nodded forward, her eyes drooped, and she fell fast asleep. Sekora curled up close beside her and purred.

***

In the hallway, a door banged and she jolted awake.

'I'll bring up the breakfast,' her mother's voice echoed from below.

Claudia stretched, still wondering what to do about the golden spring. *Jasper desperately wants me to fix the clock. But I don't need to go to London to do that!*

She leapt out of the bed and snatched her writing pad off the dressing table. She scribbled a short note to Sydney, explaining that she had found a spring that she hoped would fix the grandfather clock. Then she seized the little red box, dropped the spring inside, and ran through the door.

'Dad, would you do me a favour?'

'Depends what it is,' he said, straightening his silk tie as he walked along the hallway.

'Can you take this parcel straight to the post office?' urged Claudia. 'We can send Sydney the spring instead. If you send it first class, it'll get to him before Christmas.'

'Good idea.' Her father took the package. 'I'll drop it off on my way to work.'

'Thank you!' Claudia suddenly felt a lot more cheerful. Although she had no idea how the spring would help her. As Sekora had come back with it in his fur, and she'd dreamed about Jasper fitting it into the clock, she assumed that it must be important.

Mum came up the stairs. 'It's really cold downstairs, so I thought you might like to have your breakfast in bed,' she said, handing Claudia a tray filled with fresh fruit, eggs, bacon, sausages, and a plate piled high with hot toast.

'Thanks, Mum,' Claudia smiled. 'It looks

delicious.'

'I want to see an empty plate when I return,' her mother said, fixing her eyes on Claudia. 'You haven't been eating much lately.'

When Claudia went back into her room, Sekora was sitting on the windowsill, watching the puffins playing in the snow. She put down the tray and slumped down next to him.

'The spring has to work,' she said, remembering her dream. 'I wonder why the clock was so important to Jasper?'

Suddenly, Sekora leant back on his hind legs and started squealing. Claudia looked out of the window and gasped. Outside, amongst the dark birds, was a bright purple puffin, caught in a shower of silvery snow crystals. She stared in amazement at the unusual bird.

'I've never seen anything like it!'

Sekora pressed his paws against the window and tapped the glass.

'Do you know him?' muttered Claudia. After all the strange things that had happened around her cat, she was starting to wonder just how intelligent the animal was. Sekora stopped momentarily, only to resume tapping the glass louder and with renewed excitement.

'Maybe he lost his way in the snow.'

Claudia opened the window and the puffin swooped up towards them. He landed on the windowsill, fluffed up his feathers, and puffed out his chest. Then he started squawking and trilling like an ancient violin!

'Perhaps he's hungry.'

Claudia jumped up. She carried her breakfast tray to the windowsill, set it down, and fed some toast to the puffin. 'Here you are.'

The bird accepted the food. Sekora settled beside the purple puffin and purred, making no attempt to chase the strange bird. They seemed relaxed around each other, like domestic animals that had been raised in the same place. As Claudia passed Sekora a bit of bacon, she started to wonder if they actually knew each other. *Could they be from the same place?*

The puffin flapped his wings up and down and hopped to the edge of the windowsill.

'I'm sorry you have to go,' Claudia sighed, standing up. 'Come back and see us again soon.'

Sekora purred, his eyes fixed on the bird.

Just as the puffin went to fly away, he reached up and caught a sparkling snowflake in his beak and dropped it into Claudia's hand. 'You don't have to thank me for the food,' she said 'but maybe it'll bring me luck. I should make a wish.'

Sekora's ears pricked up. Claudia squeezed her hand shut, crushing the snowflake into fine flakes of ice, and wondered what to wish for.

I wish I could work out how to clear Daisy's name. I'll do whatever it takes, even if it means risking my life.

When Claudia opened her hand, she gave a deep shuddering gasp and glared in disbelief. The ice had formed into a key. 'Whoa! H-how did that happen…?' Her eyes grew wide in amazement as she asked, 'What does it mean?'

Sekora hissed, and swished his tail from side to side.

10

THE MAGIC DOLL'S HOUSE

Claudia had the perfect thing to keep herself busy with over the next few days.

'Now where did I put it?' she said, as she shuffled through the stack of books on the wooden shelf. 'That's it,' she yelped with delight. '*The History of Pencliff.*'

She grabbed the book, sat on her bed, and started reading about a town whose history was scarred by crime. Septimus Snail passed strict laws and severely punished people engaging in any wrongdoing. He removed the defendant's right to appeal a conviction, transferred all criminal's property over to the law, and decreed that women lose control of their property once they married. He built a gallows, installed a whipping post, and hot rods were used in the prisons to burn letters onto the skin of an offender's cheek, arm, or hand. A thief would be branded with the letter 'T', a vagrant with a 'V', and a murderer with 'M'.

During this turbulent time, the town became bitterly divided between those who agreed with the new ways, and those who were deeply opposed to them. Snail resisted any opposition to his system of law as he believed that extreme punishments would deter others from committing similar crimes. He never granted a pardon, or spared a murderer the death sentence. Every so often Claudia let out a sigh, or

43

rolled her eyes.

She also wondered whether the spring had got to Sydney safely, and if he'd been able to fix the clock.

Christmas Day dawned, cold and crisp, and sparkling fresh snow covered the trees and paths. Claudia woke to the sound of a squawking from the puffins flying around outside. She wondered if they were going to stay around forever. When she opened her eyes, she burst out laughing. Sekora was curled up next to an enormous present. It was about the height of the bed.

'What's that?' she cried, wondering if she should open it or wait for her parents to join her.

The door flew open before she could decide.

'Merry Christmas, sleepy head! I was beginning to think that you would never wake up. It's nearly ten o'clock.' Her father pulled back the curtains, letting the light flood into her room. 'I wonder who sent you such a magnificent present?' He pulled a face, as if he had no idea.

'Stop messing around!' Claudia leapt out of bed with a burst of energy. 'I know it's from you.'

'I promise you I have no idea who it's from,' said her father, straight-faced. 'It arrived yesterday afternoon in the last post and I hid it in the garage so you wouldn't see it.'

'Really?' Claudia still wasn't sure whether or not to believe her dad. She quickly untied the string, ripped off the silver wrapping paper, and her heart almost jumped from her chest.

'Wow! I don't believe it!' she squealed. 'It's the doll's house from *Splints*! But it's much smaller than I remember!' she frowned, but still looked delighted.

'I'm amazed,' her father said, open-mouthed. 'Sydney must be a very generous man. It was so light when I carried it upstairs. That's amazing!'

Claudia looked inside the house, searching for one

thing: the grandfather clock. It was ticking away at the end of the hall!

'There's a note attached to the roof, Claudia,' her dad said. 'Look!'

She took the note and it read:

The spring worked!
I thought you deserved to have this.
Merry Christmas,
Sydney.

Her dad checked his watch. 'Once you've stopped admiring your doll's house, come downstairs, OK?' As he headed through the door, they smiled at each other.

I can't believe it – it worked! Claudia stroked Sekora's silky fur. He'd come to investigate the doll's house. 'I have the doll's house and the clock – both built by Jasper!'

Sekora nuzzled his head against her cheek.

'I wonder why Jasper made the clock for the house?' Claudia climbed off the bed and carefully lifted the doll's house onto the floor. 'Maybe there's a hidden message inside somewhere, like the letter he sent.'

She searched the tiny drawers and cupboards, peeked under rugs, and behind pictures on the wall but found nothing. She was surprised that all of the small pieces of furniture had remained in place being transported from London. Then she raised her gaze to a room with a large wardrobe, spotting a toy knife glinting on the floor. She picked it up for a closer look and something strange happened.

As her hand made contact with the toy, the knife swelled in size, feeling cold and heavy, and her hand began to drip with blood. She threw it back into the house, gasping as if she'd been bewitched. Then she jumped up, grabbed a tissue from her dressing table and wiped her hand clean. She took her eyes off it for a moment, but when she looked back at the small white house, she noticed that it had also grown bigger. And it was still growing, rising up from the floor like a hot air balloon.

The roof and the walls expanded, getting stronger and thicker, and the chandeliers inside the house lit, sparkling through the sash windows. Her pulse raced, pounding in her ears, and her breathing became short and fast. Soon, her room grew at the same pace as the house. It soared above her and was so large that she could easily step inside the shiny black front door of the doll's house.

'W-what's happening?' Claudia cried out, panicky and filled with fear.

Sekora scampered through the front door.

Claudia's mind raced and she trembled from head to foot. She knew somehow that if she wanted to help Jasper she would have to enter the house. It was as if an unseen force was drawing her towards the door. She took the plunge and flew through it, feeling that something strangely magical was happening to her, and sprinted along a dimly lit hallway.

At the end of the corridor she could see a mahogany grandfather clock. Claudia skidded to a halt and looked at the antique clock. She could hear a scratching sound and a high-pitched squeal coming from the other side of the door.

Sekora's locked inside the clock! Claudia breathed deeply, desperate to set him free before something dangerous happened to them. She pushed the door, but it didn't budge. *Oh no! I can't get you out.* She tried the door again and again, but it just wouldn't open. She looked around for a key and her fingers felt around the edges of the clock, but she couldn't find one anywhere. She stared at the dial, bewildered. *A Journey in Time.*

'Hmm...' she frowned at the device and noticed

that it showed the wrong time. 'I'll start with that.' Opening the oval pane of glass that covered the face of the clock, she set the silver hands to ten o'clock, the time it was at home. The clock chimed and the hands swept smoothly and effortlessly around the dial, the little moons glowed, and the door creaked open.

'Sekora,' shouted Claudia, as she leaned inside, peering into the darkness. 'Where are you?' Her knees were trembling as if they were going to give way at any minute. She crept forward and gasped.

Inside the case of the clock, a huge brass pendulum swung to one side. The interior seemed abnormally large, as big as a room. Looking for her cat, Claudia stepped inside. She shuffled forward a few feet and spotted Sekora's pink eyes twinkling. 'There you are!' she said. 'Let's get out of here.'

The door suddenly slammed shut.

As Claudia spun around, her blood turned ice cold. She ran across the room, ducked under the pendulum, and grabbed the door handle. She frantically tried to turn it, but it was locked. She tried again, but it wouldn't budge.

'We're trapped here!' She kicked the door hard, but it still wouldn't open. 'What are we going to do now?'

Sekora's fur stood on end, his tail twitching.

Claudia was panic-stricken, desperate to find a way out. She felt hot and sticky and her skin prickled with goose bumps.

'How will we get out?'

Sekora mewed loudly and hissed.

'Maybe there's another way out,' Claudia nervously looked around the room, listening to the loud tick of the clock. She was mesmerised by the massive mechanism and a great circular moon dial that created jewel-bright patterns on the walls, like a stained-glass window. She moved closer to the heart of the clock, studying enormous toothed wheels and cogs rapidly rotating.

The next second, she heard the wind outside, wrapping itself around the clock and lifting it off the ground. The floor vibrated violently and she toppled from side to side, then stumbled back and grabbed the pendulum. Sekora slid across the floor towards her, firmly coiling his tail around her leg.

After a few bumpy moments everything fell silent and a second door on the opposite side of the clock flew open. She released the pendulum, took a deep breath, and hurried through the door with Sekora.

11

TIME TRAVEL FOR BEGINNERS

'Where am I?' Claudia's heart was beating so fast she could hardly breathe. She felt fear surge through her veins and her body shook uncontrollably. She saw before her a grand hallway with a soaring ceiling, sweeping staircase, and magnificent three-tiered crystal chandelier. *This isn't my house.*

Claudia's stomach knotted into a ball.

She ran back into the clock, ducking under the pendulum, opened the door (which offered no resistance now), and peeked out. She could see her bedroom at the end of a tunnel and realised that the clock was a portal through which she could travel to wherever she was now, and back home.

'Amazing!' she whispered excitedly.

Her bedroom was on one side and this new place was on the other. It was a magical door!

Claudia crept out of the clock on the other side, her pulse racing faster with every step, and caught sight of herself in a large gilt mirror. Instead of her pink pyjamas, she was dressed in a simple white calf-length dress with pockets, drawn together at the waist with a lilac ribbon.

How did that happen? She shook her head, as if to shake out the strange images, but when she looked again, it was still the same. Beside her, Claudia saw Sekora's pink eyes flash.

'Wait here,' Claudia whispered. 'Let me go and check it out.'

She anxiously tiptoed up the staircase and then hurried into a bedroom and closed the door. She peered around fearfully, thoroughly relieved to find that there was nobody there. The room looked old-fashioned and she couldn't see a television anywhere. It was decorated with cream wallpaper covered in pink rosebuds, and in the centre of the room was a four-poster bed, draped in velvet that cascaded between the wooden posts. She spun on her heels.

It was like she had been transported back in time. Facing her was a magnificent marble fireplace, above which hung a large oil painting of a beautiful woman in a silk ball gown, encrusted with precious gemstones.

Claudia shuffled closer. Chills raised the hairs on the back of her neck. A feeling in her stomach pulled her towards the portrait. She was intrigued by an enormous amethyst jewel sewn into the centre of the woman's bodice.

But then she shook her head and headed towards the door. *I'd better get out of here before someone comes.*

At the sound of footsteps nearing and raised voices' outside the door, Claudia stepped back into the room, and dived into a wardrobe. She crouched down, her body trembling, afraid of what might happen to her if they found a strange girl in the house. She had no idea where she was, and whether the owners would be friendly or not.

'I've already cleaned this room, Violet,' said a timid voice. 'I just need your help to change the bed linen.'

'Alright, Daisy,' said Violet. 'I don't know how you stay so cheerful with all this work.'

'It's not that bad,' Daisy replied. 'We mustn't forget to do the guest room next as the mistress is expecting a visitor first thing.'

'More work,' moaned Violet. 'How's Jasper doing?'

'He's busy working at the moment, on some sort of special commission,' Daisy sighed. 'Anyway, enough chit-chat. We need to get a move on, as the family are due back later today.'

Claudia's jaw dropped and her heart almost stopped with the shock of hearing Daisy's and Jasper's names. Could it really be her great-grandmother and great-grandfather? She wondered if the clock had transported her back in time. *Why else would she be here?*

She wanted to go out to meet Daisy, but she wasn't sure if it was the right moment, especially as that other woman – Violet – was with her. Anyway, she had no idea what she would say. They might think she was a thief, after all. How would she explain what she was doing hiding in a wardrobe? And Daisy surely wouldn't believe that Claudia was her great-granddaughter!

She bit her lip, thinking it was best to say nothing for the moment. When the two women left the room, she jumped out of the wardrobe, cautiously headed through the door, watching and listening carefully as she made her way down the stairs.

Sekora was curled up on a small sofa in the hallway.

'I won't be long,' Claudia said to the cat in a hushed voice as she opened the front door a smidgen, peeked outside, and slid through, eager to investigate further.

As Claudia descended the wide stone steps into the warm sunshine, she glanced back to be sure no-one was watching her. She was impressed to see that she had been inside a grand, white manor house with a central pillared entrance, deep sash windows, and bright red chimney pots on both sides of the roof.

Hurrying down the gravelled pathway with lawn either side, she slipped through a pair of high black gates into the street and past a row of pastel coloured town houses.

Soon, Claudia found herself heading along a sweeping road. She stared down at a golden sandy beach, backed by cliffs and views of an island in the shape of a pear. As she hurried along, the smell of the salty air filled her nostrils and she could hear waves crashing against cliffs. To one side of her, men raced about carrying boxes of fresh fruit and fish. To the other side, ladies wore white lacy blouses and ankle-length skirts, and gentlemen were in tailcoats, and cravats wrapped up to their chins.

She watched, captivated by the endless stream of passers-by who wore clothing that looked like something out of the history books she had studied at school. She tried to absorb the fact that she really had gone back in time. But what was she supposed to do here? She glanced around, wondering if it was Christmas Day here too.

'I ain't seen yer before,' said a stranger, wearing baggy trousers and a long black coat with brass buttons. 'What's yer name, Missy?'

Claudia swallowed the lump in her throat and didn't answer. She ran along the road and slipped down a cobbled alleyway, past a collection of stone cottages where she spotted two suspicious-looking men arguing. She thought she might learn more about the town, so she decided to follow them.

'But, Foggy, it's a shame we haff to split the booty with that toffee-nosed twit.'

'We got no choice, Jack,' threatened Foggy.

'S'pose yer right,' Jack grunted. 'Hey, where yer meetin' him?'

'Any minute now behind Devil Dyke Lane,' whispered Foggy. 'Percy's gonna take most of the stuff, flog it, and give us our cut.'

Jack raised one eyebrow and asked, 'D'yer trust him with the jewellery?'

'Arrrhhh... stop yer worryin',' replied Foggy, chewing the end of his cigar. 'I'll break his skull if he dun't keep his half o' the bargain.'

'S'pose yer right,' sneered Jack. 'Keep yer eye on him.'

'Better get off then,' said Foggy.

'See yer later in the *Dog and Duck.*' Jack slapped his mate hard on the back. 'I'll getta bottle o' rum in.'

'Dun't drink it all – I knows what yer like,' laughed Foggy. 'Keep us a slug.'

Claudia moved past the men swiftly like a shadow, convinced that they were up to no good. Of more concern was where she was, and why there was a portal linking this place to her house. She remembered the newspaper cutting attached to the letter that she had been sent on the morning of her birthday, and wondered if the jewellery had something to do with Jasper. But what? Maybe she could find Jasper in town.

She looked around desperately and decided to follow a couple of people, thinking that she might learn something that would help her to find Jasper, or at least understand more about where this was. Shadowing them through a dusty lane that ran between a pub and a cobbler's shop, she found herself on a grassy footpath.

'Yes, there's no doubt about it,' a stout man said. 'Leakey Porridge was a likeable rogue, who shared his ill-gotten gains with the poorest folk in the town.'

Claudia gasped, unable to believe her ears. She had read about Leakey in the history book about Pencliff. Could this be Pencliff that she was in?

'He did more good than bad,' said a shrill voice. 'Many a time I saw him delivering food and coal to the poor when it got cold.'

At the end of the path, the pair headed through a gate and disappeared inside a cottage, covered in brambles. Claudia stopped.

This is hopeless! I can't spend all day following strangers around.

She ran back down the path, turned in the direction that she hoped would lead her back to the town, but she got lost and soon found herself on the edge of a cliff. She peered around through the falling rain, shuddering with the cold.

On the summit of a steep hill, overlooking her position, she saw a medieval castle with a black flag blowing in the breeze. She gasped. On the adjacent hill was an unexpected sight. A storm cloud was hovering above a large wooden gallows from which a hangman's noose drooped, just like the one she had read about in the guide book. She also remembered the peculiar weather patterns the book talked about. *This really could be Pencliff!*

As Claudia gazed at the dangling rope, a gang of pirates with cutlasses hanging from their belts trudged past her and headed down the hill. 'Hurry up, you bunch of idiots,' said a gruff voice. 'We dun't wanna miss it.'

Cautiously, Claudia followed them. She wondered where they were going and whether Jasper might be there. She sprinted as fast as she could down the hill and into a cobbled square, fed by four narrow streets. Skidding to a halt, she glanced around. In the centre of the town was a weather-beaten bronze statue of a man on a horse, surrounded by market stalls that were selling fresh fish, fruit, and flowers. On the opposite side of the square stood rows of brightly coloured bow-fronted shops. She could see a crowd gathering outside a large, sandstone building and she walked towards it, wondering what was happening.

On the steps was a stone statue with a chipped head of Lady Justice, holding out a book entitled *Pencliff Supreme Courthouse. Pencliff…*

It has to be the same Pencliff! But how did I end up here? It's miles away. Claudia slowly stepped back. Her eyes flitted quickly over the stone structure. She thought that the building looked quite new, but she knew it had been there for nearly a hundred years.

This confirms it – I've definitely travelled back in time!

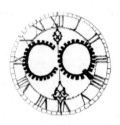

12

THE TRIAL OF LEAKEY PORRIDGE

'C'mom, yer lot,' hollered a hooligan. 'The case is bout ta start.'

Claudia joined the crowd and hurried inside the courthouse, hoping to see Jasper *somewhere* in the town. It had a dark, wooden ceiling, white marble walls, and a red cherry bench. She quickly took a seat in the public gallery, half-hidden behind a stone pillar. When the noise died down, a door flew open and a guard man-handled the prisoner into the court, bundling him into the dock. The defendant was a short, skinny man with tombstone teeth and a squint. He was wearing a ripped shirt, dirty grey trousers, and he had a bruised cheek and a cut lip.

'Stay standing, Leakey Porridge,' the guard ordered. 'If you know what's good for you.'

The court clerk stepped forward. 'All rise for the Honourable Judge Sir Septimus Snail!'

Claudia stood up and stared at the prisoner. So, this was the thief that had helped the poorest people in the town. She felt sorry for him.

The courtroom fell silent as the judge entered from his chambers and took to his high-backed leather chair. He was tall, with broad shoulders, back as straight as an arrow, and olive skin. His wavy black hair was swept back and his deep, dark eyes exuded authority and danger.

The court clerk spoke as the judge seated himself. 'This court is now in session. Today we will reach the conclusion of the case between Sir Septimus Snail, the Ruler of Pencliff, and the defendant, Leakey Porridge.'

'Everyone be seated,' the usher shouted.

The judge cleared his throat and peered at the prosecuting barrister.

'Mr Poste Slaughter,' said the judge in a strong, smooth voice, 'I am ready to hear your closing statement.'

Mr Slaughter got to his feet. 'The defendant should be found guilty of amassing a large fortune generated by engaging in stealing valuables and selling them in the taverns, Your Honour, sir.'

The judge nodded his head and then turned to the defence barrister. 'I don't need to hear from you, Mr Wright-Headed. I'm ready to pronounce the sentence.'

'As you wish, Your Honour,' sighed Mr Wright-Headed.

'This ain't a propa court,' blasted Leakey, trying to climb out of the dock. 'Where the heck's the jury?' The guard rushed forward for a second time, grabbed Leakey's arm, and roughly pushed him back into the dock.

The judge banged his gavel and scowled. 'I decide your fate!'

'Shut ya filthy mouth!' bellowed a brute sitting in front of Claudia in the public gallery. 'Ya gonna get what's coming to ya!'

'Silence in court!' the usher shouted loudly.

Claudia's face fell. She felt sympathy for Leakey, knowing that he wasn't getting a fair trial.

The judge placed a black handkerchief neatly on top of his wig.

'Leakey Porridge will be taken hence to Gallow Tree Hill, the place of execution, where he will be hanged by the neck until he is dead. Thereafter, his body will be transported to Castle Hill and drained of every drop of blood. May his twisted soul be forever banished to oblivion.'

Claudia frowned, convinced that she had misheard the judge's verdict. He couldn't be draining the defendant's body; that was barbaric.

'Your Honour.' Mr Slaughter stood up. 'I've prepared an order that any property or money that is recovered in Leakey's name is transferred directly to law – that being you.'

'Excellent,' replied the judge. 'His belongings will be sold and used to support local charities.'

Mr Slaughter gestured to the clerk of the court and handed him the order to pass to the judge. 'I have included the usual blood draining provisions for your signature.'

Draining! thought Claudia, outraged. She hadn't misheard; they were going to perform a brutal act on Leakey, and his barrister was powerless to prevent it.

'You'll pay for this!' Leakey scowled at Snail.

'I'm determined to rid this town of criminals, Porridge,' said Snail, his eyes turning ominously toward the public gallery. 'Law breakers *will* be brought to justice!'

'How sorry you'll be,' Leakey cursed the judge. 'When you and all your descendants are born blind, deaf, and dumb, 'coz that's what'll happen if you do this to me!'

Claudia shuddered at the memory of the book. She remembered reading about this very event, and here it was happening in front of her eyes!

The guard began beating Leakey with a wooden stick like he was a cake mixture. When the criminal was silenced, the guard hauled him from the court.

'Take him straight to the scaffold on Gallow Tree Hill,' ordered the judge, standing up.

Everyone hurried out of the courtroom. Claudia

desperately tried to get away but she was swept up by a rowdy crowd. She stumbled through the street amongst the rush of people and along a winding pathway that led to the hill with the gallows. Up the hill she was swept, until she was in front of the dreaded noose. It started raining. With the rain soaking her, she stared, open-mouthed, at the gallows and her body shook with fear.

'Let me out,' she cried, helplessly pushing against men's backs and chests.

'Shut up!' a scoundrel shouted with a withered eye. 'He'll be dead soon.'

When Leakey Porridge appeared, handcuffed in a cart, Claudia drew a deep breath and prayed for a miracle. Whether the man had done something wrong or not, he didn't deserve to die. The manic crowd didn't seem to agree. When he set foot next to the gallows, they went crazy, snarling like a pack of hungry dogs at their prey.

'I didn't mean to steal,' said Leakey, as he was dragged roughly up a flight of steps by a guard. 'I did it for my family.'

'It's too late,' howled a thug with a mop of red hair. 'Ya should've stayed in Scotland.'

Claudia coiled a lock of hair around her finger, pulling it hard in anger. 'C-can't you give him another chance? He did help the poor.'

'A'aaaahhh, he deserved what he got,' a brute bellowed in her face, spraying her with flecks of spit. 'There'll be no more rich pickings for Leakey.'

When the noise from the bloodthirsty mob died down, the hangman slipped the noose around Leakey's neck and squeezed it tight against his throat.

'I'll haunt the lot of you!' choked Leakey.

'We're not afraid of you!' shouted an onlooker.

The hangman pushed Leakey hard in the small of his back and he stumbled, held up by the rope around his neck.

'You can't hang me,' Leakey begged. 'Who'll look after my family?'

The hangman pulled the white cotton hood firmly over Leakey's head and then made a swift move towards the lever.

'Hang him! Hang him!' the crowd chanted.

Claudia's heart pounded and her blood turned to ice. She knew in one short minute that Leakey would be gone for good. There would be one less set of thieving hands, one less soul to walk the streets of the troubled town. Not wanting to stick around and watch the inevitable, she looked for an escape route. She stepped back, spotting a gap in the mob and made a dash for it.

As she hurried through the cobbled square the sun shone brightly, drying her hair and her clothes. And yet she was still shaking, not with the cold, but with a wave of fury. The hairs on the back of her neck stood on end as she heard a roar from the crowd somewhere behind her. The evil deed had been done. She knew this is what had happened to Daisy – or rather, what would happen to her if she didn't do something.

'If she is still working as a maid,' she muttered as she spotted the big house's red chimney pots in the distance. 'She hasn't committed any crime yet!' She now knew that Jasper had sent her here to stop the hanging. It all made sense now. Everything had led up to this. *But who would listen to a girl like me?*

Claudia rushed up the drive and silently slipped in through the unlocked front door.

She quickly picked up Sekora up from the sofa, relieved that he'd done as she had asked and stayed there. She was desperate to get home and have another look at the guide book. Pushing open the enormous grandfather clock door, she hurried inside. As she slammed the door shut, her heart leapt. Sekora jumped out of her arms and she raced across the room, grabbing a lever attached to a wheel.

Soon she could hear the wind howling horribly outside the clock and felt the floor clattering and shaking beneath her feet. Sekora dug his sharp claws into the floor and Claudia held herself steady, staring at the hands spinning wildly around the brightly lit moon dial. After several minutes there was a loud thud, the door fell open and the pendulum swung sharply to one side, allowing them to pass.

Sekora scampered out of the clock and Claudia followed him along the dimly lit hallway, through the front door of the doll's house, and into her huge bedroom. She picked Sekora up, lovingly stroking the crescent-moon patch of fur on his head, and gently placed him on her bed.

She turned around, watching in amazement as the enormous white house shuddered, shrank, and sank to the floor. The house was getting smaller and smaller, the lights dimming in the windows, and the chimney pots stopped smoking. Within a minute, the house was back to its original size, as was her room.

'Unbelievable,' Claudia said, sinking into her bed. She grabbed the book on Pencliff, but as she started to read it the door opened and her mother walked into the room.

'What have you been doing?' Her mother's voice rose. 'And why is your hair so messy?'

'Err...'

'Well?' her mother insisted.

Claudia paused. Panic rushed through her as she struggled for an explanation. She must have looked a mess. How was she going to talk her way out of this?

13

FROZEN IN TIME

'Err… nowhere,' Claudia said, her mind racing for answers. 'I was just playing with the doll's house.' Claudia dropped the book on her bed. 'I'll give my hair a quick brush.'

'Good idea, but don't be too long. Breakfast is almost ready.' Looking sceptical, her mum left the room.

Claudia stared at the clock in disbelief. It was still ten o'clock! Time must have stopped here while she was in Pencliff. She looked down to find that she was back in her pink pyjamas.

She rushed downstairs and bolted her breakfast, barely speaking to her parents. She couldn't wait to get back upstairs, and have a soak in the bath and think about what had just happened to her.

After Claudia had washed her hair, she retraced every step she took in Pencliff. She closed her eyes and allowed her mind to wander, oblivious of how long she lay in the bath.

'Lunch is ready!' her mother shouted up the stairs.

Claudia realised that she'd fallen asleep in the bath. She hurried into her bedroom, towel-dried her long curly hair, tied it up in a red ribbon, and quickly got dressed. Then she gestured Sekora to follow her and they raced downstairs, jumping two at a time, and headed across the hall.

As Claudia entered the dining room, her stomach started growling. The table was full of dishes piled high with food. There were so many things that she loved: roast potatoes, boiled potatoes, pigs in blankets, Yorkshire puddings, sprouts, buttered peas, rich gravy, and a huge turkey decorated with holly.

'What have you been doing?' her father asked, pulling out a chair for her to sit down next to him.

'N-nothing,' Claudia stuttered, thinking about Pencliff. 'I've been rearranging the doll's house.' She picked up a gold-foiled cracker and waved it in his face. 'Pull it,' she said, trying to act normally, even though her mind was on Daisy. It popped, and out fell a black, rubbery spider that wriggled across the table. She picked it up and threw it on the floor for Sekora to play with.

'I hate spiders,' said Claudia, as her mother laid down a plate of food on the floor for Sekora. 'Can you tell me anything about Pencliff, Dad?'

'It's a beautiful old town near the coast,' he said nodding his head nostalgically, 'but I haven't been there for years, and I don't really know much about its history.'

'Did they have any odd traditions?' Claudia was thinking about the hangings.

'Never heard of any.' He picked up the carving knife and cut thick slices of turkey.

'Why, what have you read?'

'It used to have public hangings.'

'Really?' said her mother, passing the peas around.

Her father grunted disapprovingly. 'They certainly were cruel in the old days.'

'Will you take me there after Christmas?' Claudia asked, helping herself to more roast potatoes. 'I've got a family tree project to complete over the holidays. I haven't got a problem with that. Although, I don't have any family living there now.' He raised his glass.

'By the way, Merry Christmas, everyone!'

After dinner, Claudia was keen to return to her room. 'I'll be in my bedroom if you want me,' she said, beckoning Sekora to come with her. He looked up from the spider and leapt to Claudia's heels as she stood up. 'I'll see you both later.'

'You haven't even opened our presents yet!' her mum said, to her back. She couldn't think about any other presents. She needed to look through the book on Pencliff and work out her next move. Sprinting into her bedroom, she grabbed the book, sat on her bed, and started reading the final chapter.

She discovered that Dorcas, a woman who was thought to be a sorceress, settled in the town with her puffin and befriended a stray cat, who was highly intelligent and could communicate with humans. Dorcas became disenchanted with the way the town was being run. She spoke out against the despicable hangings and it was alleged that her actions restored life to those who had been wronged.

Now that Claudia knew about Jasper's time-travelling clock, she was convinced that somehow Jasper had left this book on the train for her. She had actually visited the past, so maybe Jasper could come to the present.

With Daisy living in the doll's house, the only explanation Claudia could think of was that Jasper had created the doll's house and a time-travelling machine in the hope that he could transport someone back to clear Daisy's name. But why couldn't Jasper do it himself?

It seemed crazy but almost everything that had happened since Claudia had received Jasper's letter was a little bit crazy. It was almost too much to fit into her brain, but she had to keep going.

She also considered the possibility that if time travel was real, what else was real? What's to say that a sorceress, like Dorcas was said to be, wasn't real as well?

Claudia closed the book. It was all very confusing, but she had to plan her next move. She realised that she didn't just have to clear Daisy's name; she also had to do it in a town controlled by Snail, a merciless man who ruled with an iron fist.

'That won't stop me,' she muttered to herself. 'I've got to do it. For Jasper.'

Sekora's ears perked up and he wagged his tail. He seemed to agree.

14

A BOY CALLED HUGO

'Claudia? Aunty Annabelle just rang. She wants us to go over for a few hours,' the soft voice of Claudia's mother came through the partially-opened bedroom door.

'OK. I'll be down in a moment.'

She hadn't enjoyed opening her presents as her head was still buzzing with questions about Pencliff. She knew she needed to stop worrying about Daisy and what she would say when she met her. Thinking of this, she grabbed her coat and headed out, calling, 'See you later, Sekora.'

Claudia had a lovely Christmas Day evening at her Aunty's house. She sat in the living room, next to a roaring fire, admiring the twinkling lights on the Christmas tree. Every time her parents spoke about their trip to London, and how Sydney Splint had gifted Claudia a doll's house and a clock for Christmas, she grinned. She knew that they would never believe that the doll's house was a real home, and that the clock was a time-travelling machine.

After they tucked into a tea of turkey sandwiches, strawberry trifle, and fruit cake jam-packed with cherries and nuts, Claudia felt sleepy and was ready to leave.

When they arrived home, Claudia headed straight to her bedroom. Sekora was curled up on her comfy chair, fast asleep. Claudia tiptoed across the room, put on her pink pyjamas, and climbed into bed. She snuggled down beneath the duvet and then sighed heavily. She still didn't know what to do about Daisy.

***

Boxing Day dawned, cold and frosty. Claudia woke at eight, feeling too restless to go back to sleep. Her breath clouded around her in the freezing air. She got up, put on her towelling robe, and went straight into the bathroom for a long hot shower to clear her head. When she returned to her room, feeling refreshed, she dragged on her jeans and jumper.

Claudia suddenly realised that Sekora was missing. She checked in her wardrobe and under her bed, but he wasn't there. This time she wasn't worried, she knew he would return. They had a special connection, she was sure of it.

Instead, she worried about Daisy. She paced up and down the room, deep in thought, wondering what she should do.

I'll have to go back alone!

She felt braver with Sekora by her side but there was nothing else for it. It was only a matter of time before Daisy lost her freedom, and her life. Claudia knew she had to act fast.

Standing in front of the doll's house, she bravely pushed open the front door. Abruptly, it started to quiver and quake, the black roof expanded, the chimney pots shot into the air, and it grew up from the floor, getting larger and larger and more lifelike. As the lights in the windows flashed, she dashed through the front door and along the carpeted corridor until she reached the clock. She quickly checked her watch, opened the glass pane, and set the hands to eight o'clock. The moons glowed, the hands started spinning wildly around and the clock sprung to life.

As the door creaked open, the pendulum swung

aside and she hopped inside. She held her breath, feeling a little nervous without Sekora, but she knew she had to keep going if she wanted to help Daisy. *Who knows how much time I have left?*

She pressed her body tight against the wall, listening to the chimes ringing in her ears. The floor started trembling beneath her feet and, for several minutes, the marvellous mechanical clock whirled and twirled around.

'Now,' said Claudia aloud. As the door opened, she stepped out and said, 'I need to speak to Daisy.' She hesitated for a moment, thinking about how she would explain who she was, or how she knew that Daisy was in danger.

'Happy Halloween!' The greeting startled Claudia, making her jump. 'I'm so pleased to meet you.'

Claudia quickly spun around. 'H-hello,' she stammered

'Hello, Miss. I'm Hugo Hamilton-Barnes,' the boy in front of her said, breaking into a wide smile. 'Dorcas told us that you were coming to stay while your parents were away on business.'

Claudia recovered from the shock and stepped closer, searching his face. *Who is this? And who does he think I am? And why would Dorcas be expecting me?*

Hugo had straight blond hair that fell partly across one side of his face, and forget-me-not blue eyes that were as cool and calm as the sound of his posh voice.

'Do you know her well?' Hugo asked.

'Not really,' gulped Claudia, thinking on her feet. 'She's a… close friend of a relative of mine.'

'Any friend of Dorcas is a friend of mine.' Hugo's face lit up. 'She's an amazing sorceress who has the power to control the weather. Of course it doesn't always work, especially if there's a strong breeze at sea.'

Claudia's jaw dropped and her eyes widened in disbelief. The sorceress in the guide book. Could that be real, too? If so, would Dorcas be expecting her in particular?

Hugo must have seen the surprised look on Claudia's face.

'You didn't know she was a sorceress?' Hugo said quickly.

Claudia nervously shook her head. 'N-no, I'm afraid not. I've never actually met her before.' *Well, at least that isn't a lie.*

'Oh, well, I don't suppose it matters. It's not a secret! Dorcas comes from a powerful family of magicians.'

Claudia gazed at him in disbelief. The matter-of-fact way in which he talked about a person with magical powers was dumbfounding. She hadn't thought about it before, but Jasper must have been technically gifted to be able to create a time-travelling clock. Was that magic, too?

'Do you have any magical powers?' Hugo asked.

'Err... you're kidding? There's nothing special about me.' Claudia let out a laugh and then a sudden thought crossed her mind. She wondered if she had inherited any of Jasper's abilities, but quickly dismissed the idea as ridiculous. After all, she would have known if she had magic powers!

Hugo raised an eyebrow. 'What does "kidding" mean?'

'It's just an expression we use at home.' Claudia's face flushed pink. 'It means you must be joking.'

'Would you like to have a look around the town?' suggested Hugo, heading for the door.

'That'd be awesome.' Claudia followed him out, intrigued to learn more about the town.

'Awesome?' Hugo shook his head, smiled, and said, 'Some people say the strangest things.'

As they descended the wide stone steps into Upper Puffin Place, Claudia heard a cat squeal. She quickly turned around, recognising the sound immediately. *Sekora!* He was scampering along a low stone wall. Claudia smiled and felt a wave of relief swirl inside her. She guessed that he was quite happy to go back and forth between modern day Pettifog and old Pencliff. Although she hoped that he would still be her pet when she was home.

'Are you alright?' Hugo looked at the cat and frowned.

'Yes, I'm fine,' said Claudia.

Claudia kept walking, enjoying the sunshine. She decided that it was best not to mention her previous visit to the town.

As they headed along a curving road, a cold, biting wind cut between the buildings. Claudia glanced around, instantly recognising the golden sandy beach and the view of the pear-shaped island.

'What's that island called?'

'That's Rat Island,' Hugo replied, as she followed him into a narrow alleyway sandwiched between brightly coloured, three-storey houses.

'What are you doing here?' a man asked, staring at Claudia. He was descending a flight of steep steps of a pale blue house.

As Claudia came to a halt, a cold chill slid down her spine and the hair on the nape of her neck stood on end. It was the dangerous Judge Snail from the courthouse. She wondered why he wanted to talk to her. As anxiety rose in her throat, she struggled to get out of the way. *What does he know about me?*

15

SIR SEPTIMUS SNAIL

'Hello, Hugo. How are you?'

'Hello, Uncle,' said Hugo, smiling. 'I'm fine.'

Claudia released the breath she'd been holding. She realised that he wasn't talking to her. He had just seen his nephew.

'Meet Claudia,' Hugo said in a friendly voice. 'She's staying with us for a few days while her parents are away.'

'Hello' Claudia said, looking uncomfortable. She couldn't help remembering how ruthless he'd been in court.

'Sorry, I can't stop, Hugo.' He nodded to Claudia and simply said, 'Claudia,' as he kept walking. Then he said, 'I have urgent business to attend to.'

'He's always busy working,' Hugo said once he was out of earshot.

Claudia pretended that she'd never seen him before. 'Who is he?'

'Sir Septimus Snail. He's the ruler of this town.'

By the time they reached the cobbled square, the wind had dropped and it felt warmer.

'It's certainly a nice place.' Claudia glanced around the town centre as though she hadn't seen the bronze statue of Ambrose, or the market stalls before.

'Here's Arnold Leech,' Hugo said, as a cigar-shaped man with busy eyebrows and coarse, salt and pepper hair headed towards them. 'That's odd. What he's doing in town at this time of day? He's usually working at the house about now.'

'Good morning, Master Hugo.'

'Are you looking for us, Arnold?' Hugo asked, confused.

'Yes, I've been searching for you everywhere,' Arnold replied strictly. 'Lady Puckett would like to see you as soon as you return to the house.'

'Don't worry, Arnold, we'll go straight there,' said Hugo. 'This is Claudia. She'll be staying with us for a while. I was just showing her around first.'

'Pleased to meet you.'

Arnold politely tilted his head in her direction. 'If you need anything at all, don't hesitate to ask.'

'Thank you,' Claudia smiled.

'See you later, Arnold.' Hugo waved his hand and they wandered past the market stalls. 'I'm amazed that he didn't ask one of the other servants to deliver the message.'

'He seems nice,' Claudia said.

'Arnold is a fine man who has served my family for many years. But he won't stand for any nonsense.'

AAARRKARR-OO-ARR!

Claudia swung around, her ears ringing. 'What's that sound?'

'It's the puffins of Pencliff,' Hugo howled with laughter. 'They're magical little creatures.'

Claudia noticed a small flock of puffins had landed on the statue. They were just like the ones at home – striking clown-like birds with brightly coloured beaks and a comical hop in their walk. She remembered the purple puffin and wondered if he ever made it home.

'They transport potions and messages around the town, and back and forth between the islands, for Dorcas,' explained Hugo.

'They're amazing.' Claudia was thinking what her mum said about them delivering her birthday cards. 'What were you telling me about Rat Island?'

'It was once an unspoilt place, famous for its gemstones. But now it's where the town puts its strongest thieves and other criminals.'

Claudia sensed his sadness. 'Why are the prisoners sent there?'

'To dig for rare stones, which are sold abroad to support the town,' said Hugo. 'Other criminals are thrown into the local jail. Or hung.'

Claudia stiffened. A disturbing image of Daisy standing in the dock flashed through her mind. She could even hear a voice in her ear shouting, 'Guilty!'

'Are you alright?' Hugo stared at Claudia. She felt woozy.

'I'm fine,' said Claudia, shaking her head. 'Do you have any other family apart from your grandmother, and of course your uncle, living here?'

'Lady Agatha is my aunt. She's my mother's sister. She's married to Uncle Septimus.' Hugo nodded and proudly puffed out his chest. 'She's a fine-mannered lady who works tirelessly for the poor.'

They wandered to the end of the street and stopped for a moment to admire the view of a beach. It was sheltered by a large harbour that bustled with boats. Hugo pointed to a grand stone structure with tall, circular towers that merged with the jagged cliff. It was covered in sparkling snow and over-run with ivy vines that climbed the walls and wound their way around the windows.

'That's Chillingbone Castle, where uncle Septimus lives,' said Hugo.

'It's amazing,' said Claudia, thinking of the snow back home. She studied the castle for a moment, wondering what went on behind those closed windows. Why did it make her feel so uncomfortable?

16

ST AGATHA'S ISLAND

Mist rolled in from the sea as Claudia and Hugo headed through a moss-covered archway to a coastal track. At the same time the wind blew stronger, and a fine drizzle began to fall.

'I'm freezing,' shuddered Claudia.

Hugo stopped and leant on the wall beside her. She glanced around. A large island with a fort and an enormous iron door embedded into its rocky cliff-face caught her eye. It lay just a short distance from the beach, and would have been surrounded by the sea whenever the tide came in.

'What's that place?'

'That's St Agatha's island. It was named after my aunty to commemorate her birth,' Hugo said. 'The fort was once a lavish house where Ambrose lived with his family.'

As Claudia strained to see through the mist and drizzle, eerie whimpering cries echoed through the murkiness.

'What's that noise?'

'The townsfolk that are trapped in the sea jail,' said Hugo with a sullen face.

'Sea jail? What did they do wrong?'

'They spoke out against the law,' Hugo replied, 'or they stirred up trouble in the town and refused to pay their taxes. Everyone who does that is arrested and slung into the sea jail.'

Claudia gulped.

'My uncle is a stickler for law and order.'

A violent storm was brewing around them, blowing the mist away from the shore. In the distance, a sail boat appeared and started to rock hard from side to side. Just then, a bolt of lightning struck the mast, snapping it in two and the strong wind pushed the boat away around the headland.

'What's my uncle doing in the fort?' muttered Hugo. 'I hope that there hasn't been any trouble.'

On St Agatha's island, Claudia could see Snail running down the wide stone steps, raising his arms at the sea.

'What's happening?'

'Look!' cried Hugo, as he leant over the wall. 'There are prisoners being led across the sand.'

Claudia's eyes widened in horror and her pulse raced. A horde of ragged men and women shuffled along the beach. They looked confused and exhausted. She watched as the sea started swirling around them, and giant waves broke on the shore. The clouds darkened and flashes of lightning zig-zagged across the sky.

Rising from the swelling sea were columns of black smoke that swirled into human-shaped silhouettes with bulging red eyes and eagle's wings. They took off and flew over the choppy waves, wailing and howling like hungry wolves. Once they reached the frothy shore, they grabbed the prisoners by the scruff of their necks, turned to the island, and threw them into the sea.

'What are they?' Claudia froze to the spot and fear flashed through her.

'They are the sea spirits that drive the prisoners into the cave beneath the island.'

'Why?' she asked in a panicky voice.

75

'So they can be transmogrified into cytoplasmic hybrids,' Hugo said with a sullen face.

'Err… cytoplasmic whats?' Claudia had absolutely no idea what Hugo was talking about.

'They are people that have been condemned to live in the bodies of sea creatures,' Hugo explained. 'When they enter the cave, the jailor pours a shape-shifting potion into the water that transforms parts of their bodies into those of sea creatures.'

Claudia gasped. *What kind of place was Pencliff? Magic seemed to be everywhere.*

Snail was shouting at the prisoners now; 'That's what happens when you break the law!'

The sea spirits released the huge iron gate in the cliff side, and drove the prisoners into the sea jail. Hugo stepped away from the wall. 'We'd better get going,' he said. 'I promised that we'd go straight home. But there are still a couple more places I want to show you first.'

Claudia just nodded, too stunned to speak. As the two of them ran around the rocky outcrop and past Pencliff Castle, the weather calmed down and the sun broke through the fluffy clouds.

'Snail's really powerful,' blurted Claudia, as her normal heart rate returned. 'Is he like Dorcas?'

'Yes, he's a sorcerer too,' Hugo replied. 'Although he's different from Dorcas. They have different powers and beliefs.'

Claudia felt shaky after what she had just witnessed and she realised that she would have to be very careful what she did or she might end up being slung into the sea jail. *I've got to warn Daisy to get out of town! It's the only way. But why would she believe me?*

As they wandered along the path, Claudia's pulse returned to normal. She stopped and stared at a large stone house perched on top of a cliff that jutted out over a cove.

'Why's that place all boarded up?'

'That's Thomas Truscott's ancestral home. He took over the estate from his parents when they decided to move into town.'

'It looks really run down.'

'Thomas recklessly gambled away his fortune, and turned to a life of crime,' Hugo said glum-faced. 'He spent his nights flashing a lantern from the shore, beckoning ships and driving them into the cliffs, so he could salvage the cargo.'

'That's awful! What happened to him?'

'One night, he headed towards the wreckage, unaware that his insatiable greed would end in tragedy. To his horror, lying amongst the dead bodies was his beloved father, Captain Charles Truscott.'

'Look, Hugo, the boat we saw hit by lightning has crashed into the rocks!' Claudia saw a gaping gash in the hull, which quickly filled with water, causing it to list to one side and sink. As the sea swallowed up the boat and its occupants, all that was left were wooden crates bobbing up and down on the swell. Claudia felt sick with anguish at the thought of those poor people who must have drowned.

'Look! There's Thomas now.' Hugo pointed at man in a navy coat and long black boots who appeared on the beach, riding a white horse that shimmered in the sunlight. He was followed by men driving horse-drawn carts and carrying nets and chains.

'Oh no, they're too late.'

Standing on the neck of Thomas's horse, controlling the reins, were small, bright blue spirits with wrinkled faces and big ears.

Claudia's jaw dropped. 'What are they?'

'The water spirits that ensure Thomas can never escape his punishment,' Hugo told her.

Claudia dropped her voice to a mere whisper. 'It's worse than death.' She watched the spirits steer the horse towards the edge of the sea and stop.

'All that's left is the cargo,' Hugo said sadly.

The men jumped off the carriages, grabbed the heavy nets and waded through the water up to their waists. Roughly throwing the nets over the crates, they hauled them to the shore.

'What's happening?' asked Claudia as a man tore open a box, rummaged through the contents and pulled out a small silver casket.

'Thomas has to ride the sea tunnels,' said Hugo, 'and deliver the treasure straight to my uncle's castle.'

'Why?'

'Any unclaimed cargo is sold and the money is used towards building a lifeboat station,' Hugo said cheerily. 'It'll save many lives.'

'That's great.' Claudia nodded her head and smiled, happy to hear some good news.

'This way,' said Hugo gesturing Claudia to follow him. 'Let's go to South Beach next.'

Once they reached the end of the winding pathway, they raced down the steep stone steps that led to a long, sandy beach, sheltered by high cliffs.

'South Beach stretches from St Agatha's Island to Hunter's Leap.' Hugo's eyes darted around quickly and settled on a large rock a little distance away. 'At low tide, you can cross to Hunter's Leap, and see the spectacular Cave of Crystals.'

'I'd love to visit the caves.' Claudia forgot for a moment what she was doing there. She added, 'But I'm not sure how long I'll be able to stay.'

'Stay as long as you like,' Hugo said. 'It's nice to have some company for a change.'

'I will,' replied Claudia, thinking it was going to be harder than she first thought to help Daisy with all that she had seen of the town.

'Dorcas often visits Hunter's Leap and collects the crystals,' said Hugo. 'Her house is full of them.'

'What does she do with them?'

'She likes to examine them,' Hugo replied. 'She says that they hold the key to the past.'

'I've never heard of that before.'

They climbed the sand dunes and quickly made their way up a steep hill back into town, and along winding streets until they reached Lower Puffin Place.

'Here we are!' said Hugo. Stopping, he pointed at a large house that seemed different to all of the others in the area.

'Who lives there?' Claudia asked.

'One of the most powerful people you will ever meet.'

17

MEETING THE LOCALS

Claudia's spine shivered at the sight of the house. It made her hesitate before approaching, as if it was sending out a warning. Something powerful resided within these walls.

'It's Dorcas's house,' Hugo said in a cheery voice.

So that was why she felt uneasy, the house was magic. As they walked towards the three-storey stone building, with its tall, black door and puffin-shaped knocker, Claudia's stomach flipped. She was worried about meeting Dorcas and what she might say to her.

As Hugo mounted the narrow steps, the door flew open, and a puffin with a message hanging from its beak whooshed past his head.

'Watch out,' he warned Claudia, ducking. 'It's probably a delivery for Rat Island.'

Claudia giggled and followed Hugo into a dimly lit room with a smouldering fire and heavy wooden beams lining the ceiling. Instantly, sweet-scented candles mysteriously started to ignite, one by one, and the room brightened. Hugo smiled seeing Claudia's look of wonder, and said, 'It's alright, Dorcas was expecting me.'

Claudia was struck by the sheer size of the place and in particular the mahogany cabinets that stretched from floor to ceiling. They were lined with shelves of great glass jars, some overflowing with sparkling crystals of every size, shape, and colour. It was mesmerising.

'Take a look around,' encouraged Hugo. 'Dorcas won't mind.'

Claudia inched towards a rugged oak table. It was laden with dried flowers, a cauldron full of strong-smelling herbs, a collection of ancient maps, and a large purple pot bubbling away, without a flame. Above her head, beech-handled brooms were tied to the beams.

'The townsfolk keep brooms in their homes for protection,' said Hugo, following Claudia's gaze upwards. 'They use them to sweep away meddlesome spirits. We have one at home too, though I'm not sure how much the maids use it. My mother and father would though – they believe in the powers of good and bad spirits.'

Claudia's eyes settled on another corner, where a striking crystal moon globe gleamed brightly on a shelf. She moved closer. It was covered in swirly silver symbols that she couldn't understand.

'Dorcas told me that it was created in the last century by a selenologist for the first moon sorceress,' said Hugo knowledgeably. 'Dorcas's power is linked to the mystical moon phases on the globe.'

Claudia shuddered. 'Brrr… I'm freezing.'

'Dorcas keeps this part of the house much cooler,' said Hugo, rubbing his hands in agreement, 'to preserve the precious globe.'

Suddenly, a crackling noise erupted in the room. The fire roared in the grate, and purple-blue flames shot from the logs, spitting sparks onto the old oak floor. To Claudia's surprise, the solid stone fireplace slid to one side, allowing Dorcas to step into the room. She was a statuesque figure, with lavender eyes, long flaming red hair, and a flowing black cloak.

'You never know where she'll come from,'

muttered Hugo, grinning at Claudia's astonished expression.

'I'm glad you came,' said Dorcas in a deep and mysterious voice. 'Please, take a seat.'

She gestured to the wooden stools nearby. 'Jasper told me that you might be coming, and asked me if I might arrange for you to stay with Hugo's family.'

Claudia's face lit up. *So coming here was in his plan all along!* 'Do you see much of Jasper?'

'As much as I can,' Dorcas replied. 'Although, I haven't seen him lately, as he's busy working at the castle for Cousin Septimus.'

'What's he doing for him?' asked Claudia. *I'm not sure I like the sound of Jasper working for Septimus.* She had a bad feeling, a really bad feeling.

'I'm not sure, but you know how talented he is. I expect it's something mechanical,' said Dorcas.

'Maybe he's making a clock,' suggested Claudia.

Dorcas shook her head. 'I wouldn't have thought so. There are enough clocks in the castle.'

She wondered why he had written to her from a prison cell and she hoped that he wasn't in any danger. After what she'd seen about the way prisoners were dealt with, she was afraid for him now.

'I've been showing Claudia around the town,' Hugo explained.

'What do you think of Pencliff?' Dorcas enquired with a wide smile.

'It's a really nice place... err... apart from the spirits.'

'I agree,' Dorcas nodded. 'There are far too many of them.'

'Unfortunately, my uncle is afraid of losing control of the town,' said Hugo.

'Hugo's right. Cousin Septimus believes that there is a lot of bad blood in the town and he has summoned spirits to maintain law and order,' said Dorcas.

'Occasionally, I disagree with my cousin and use my power to defeat them. With the help of my supporters, of course.'

Claudia's heart skipped. It sounded dangerous.

'I have a walk planned tonight, in fact, and I need all the help I can get.'

'Don't worry, we'll both be there,' said Hugo, catching Claudia's eye.

'I would be most grateful.'

Claudia took a big gulp and nodded sheepishly. She had no idea what she was getting herself into.

***

Once they had returned to Upper Puffin Place, Arnold greeted Hugo and Claudia at the front door.

'Don't forget, Hugo,' said Arnold, 'your grandmother wishes to see you in the upstairs drawing room.'

'Yes, thank you Arnold,' Hugo said.

'How do you like our town, Claudia?' Arnold enquired.

'Very much, thanks.'

'Would you like to meet my grandmother, Claudia?' asked Hugo. 'She's celebrating her eightieth birthday today.'

'I'd love to!'

They sped up the stairs and along the landing towards a servant, who neatly stepped aside and opened the door. Claudia stared at the servant, disappointed that it wasn't Daisy.

'By the way,' Hugo said, suddenly stopping and pointing his finger, 'your room is at the end of this corridor, marked with a number six.'

'Thanks,' Claudia said, wondering if she'd really be expected to stay here overnight. At least no time would be passing at home while she was away. At least she hoped not. What would happen if it didn't stop, her parents would be frantic looking for her. She dismissed the thought. *There's nothing I can do about that now, I have to find Daisy.*

'Here she is,' said Hugo, rushing across the room to greet his grandmother.

Claudia was captivated by the grand room. It had pale blue walls, gilt mirrors, velvet sofas, and a vast view of the sea. The table near the window was covered with brightly coloured birthday cards, and a pile of presents as tall as Claudia.

Lady Puckett was an endearing old lady with a kind face, who appeared far younger than her eighty years. She was relaxing in an armchair, reading. Claudia thought it looked like a telegram. She'd seen one like it in a museum once.

'This is Claudia,' said Hugo cheerfully. 'She's staying with us for a while.'

'Happy Birthday, Lady Puckett,' Claudia said politely, but warmly. 'I hope it's OK for me to stay?'

'Thank you, my dear,' said Lady Puckett. 'It's nice to meet you. And of course, any friend of Hugo is most welcome at the house.'

'Are you looking forward to your party?' asked Hugo.

'Yes,' said Lady Puckett, smiling, 'we have a lot of important people arriving this evening.'

Hugo kissed her on the cheek. For a moment Claudia wondered whether she should too, and then thought better of it.

'Is it alright if Claudia comes tonight too?'

'Of course, she must come,' replied Lady Puckett. 'Everyone is welcome to celebrate with me.'

'Thank you,' said Claudia. Her hopes rose, thinking that the party could be the perfect chance to speak to Daisy.

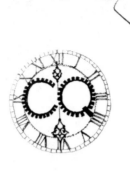

18

THE SPIRIT WALK

By six o'clock, it was already getting dark. Claudia could see the gleam of the moon on the jagged coastline. She followed Hugo through a twisty alleyway and emerged into a cobbled courtyard that led to the Tudor Merchant's House, as Hugo explained. It was sandwiched between a row of stone cottages and an old bookshop. Opposite the historic house was a large tree with branches that looked like reptiles' tails.

Claudia was getting worried that she wouldn't bump into Daisy at the house.

'So what exactly will happen on this spirit walk?' she asked, a little concerned as they neared the event.

'Dorcas will use her powers, and those of her followers,' said Hugo, 'to try to undo the past.'

'What does your uncle think about it?'

'He won't be happy about it. But what can he do? Dorcas is a force to be reckoned with, that even Uncle Septimus would think twice about challenging.'

Something caught Claudia's eye and she asked, 'What's that light twinkling in that tree?'

'Dorcas summoned a spirit boy and his dog to live there,' Hugo explained. 'He watches the house and reports any ships that dock in the harbour. My uncle has tried to get rid of him. He made an order that the tree should be set on fire, but it wouldn't burn.'

'I bet that made him angry,' said Claudia.

'I heard that the dog jumped onto the man's shoulders when he lit the torch and bit his neck,' laughed Hugo. 'He'll have certainly learnt a lesson from that.'

'Who used to live here?' Claudia turned her head towards the house.

'Igneous Stuart,' said Hugo. 'His skull is still buried in the herb garden at the back of the house. If you dig it up on Halloween at the stroke of midnight and place a corpse candle inside, you'll see the next person to be hung.'

'There's no way I'd be able to look,' said Claudia in horror, 'in case I saw my own face.'

'*Hopefully*, that won't happen to either of us,' said Hugo, not so reassuringly. 'Anyway, we won't have time to dig it up tonight – we have to get back for the party.'

The old oak door of the Tudor Merchant's House creaked open and a shabby boy no higher than a broomstick appeared. He had a bony face, dull grey eyes, and a ruddy complexion.

'Hello, Scraggy,' said Hugo. 'All ready for tonight?'

'Yes,' answered Scraggy. 'Although, who knows what might happen?'

'That's true,' said Hugo as Scraggy dashed off.

'Who's he?' asked Claudia.

'Dorcas's companion. He helps her to organise the spirit walk and keeps a look out for harmful spirits.'

Claudia felt her arms prickling with goose bumps.

'Dorcas isn't here yet,' said Hugo glancing around, 'but would you like a quick look at the house?'

Claudia nodded.

They scuttled inside. It was a dark, cold place and the wind whistled an eerie tune in the chimney. Claudia was mesmerised. She cast her eyes over the heavy timber beams, coats of arms, white-washed walls with enormous tapestries, and the stone fireplace with a large black cooking pot hanging in it.

'Meet the Stuarts,' said Hugo, moving towards a tapestry of a large family feasting around the dinner table. They stopped eating, looked up, and started waving their hands.

Claudia was amazed by the moving tapestry.

'Are you joining us tonight, Igneous?' asked Hugo.

'Scraggy brought a bowl of fennel seeds,' said Igneous, stepping out of the fabric. 'He asked me to sprinkle them around the gates of the graveyards tonight, to ward off the prankster spirits.'

Hugo sighed heavily. 'Those spirits are known for nailing front doors shut, taking gates off hinges, breaking windows, and starting fires.'

'Why?' Claudia asked, staring at Igneous in disbelief.

Hugo didn't answer. He moved to an old chest and a wooden bowl and started running his hands through the seeds. 'Hopefully, these seeds will stop the spirits escaping the graveyard.'

Claudia shot across the room to stand beside him.

'We'd better be off,' said Hugo, heading for the door. 'Good luck, Igneous.'

They hurried down the steps and joined a steady stream of people carrying lanterns who were pouring into the courtyard. They were dressed in dark clothes, and mumbling and nodding amongst themselves.

'She'll be here any minute,' said Hugo.

As Claudia looked at the alleyway leading to Dorcas's house, a purple mist billowed into the square, curling around the crowd. Once it cleared, Dorcas could be seen heading through the crowd and then standing on the steps of the Tudor Merchant's House.

Claudia gasped.

'Hail Dorcas! Hail Dorcas!' the crowd chanted.

'Our heroine!' shouted a stout man with curly hair.

Dorcas waved to her followers, and said gratefully, 'Thank you, dear friends.'

Scraggy pushed past people from the back of the crowd, coming to stand beside Dorcas. Then he pulled a bell from his pocket and rung it several times.

'What's he doing?' whispered Claudia.

'He's purifying the air,' said Hugo, 'and banishing any bad spirits in the area.'

'Welcome to my spirit walk,' said Dorcas in a deep and powerful voice that demanded attention. 'In these dark days, we stand together, ready to banish bad spirits from our shores,' her voice rose. 'Working together we have the power to undo the past.'

Dorcas pointed her finger in the direction of Gallow Tree Hill. 'The hangman's noose casts a shadow over each and every one of us.'

The crowd groaned and some of the people shook their fists.

'Tonight,' said Dorcas, 'we will restore dreams and release the townsfolk trapped beneath the cave!'

The crowd cheered, stamped their feet, and applauded loudly.

'Come with me!' said Dorcas, beckoning her followers.

The crowd pushed forward, following her towards one of the alleyways off the square. At the end of a long lane they turned and then walked purposefully up Castle Hill.

'Where are we going?' Claudia asked Hugo.

'To face the dead.'

Claudia's heart pounded in her ears.

At the top of the hill Dorcas stopped abruptly and glared at Pencliff Castle. The frothy sea surged forward, then rapidly retreated, hissing and seething back into the darkness, as if it was full of evil spirits. The crowd nervously huddled together and fell silent.

'Leakey Porridge!' bellowed Dorcas.

A strangled cry rang out.

'Reveal yourself,' cried Dorcas, 'or remain a spirit until the end of time!'

Suddenly, an enormous black shadow loomed out of the gloom of the castle wall like a great tower. Then it shrank in size and materialised into a man with acid green eyes. The crowd gasped and retreated a few steps as one.

Claudia's whole body trembled with fear.

'Get away from here!' yelled Leakey, as he tore at the tangled rope still tied around his neck. 'I know I did wrong, picking the pockets of people close to me, but I never harmed a living soul, and I shared what I stole with the poorest folk in town.'

'I'm here to help you, Leakey,' Dorcas said, moving closer with a thoughtful look on her face, 'and return you to the arms of your family.'

'If only that were possible,' Leaky said sadly.

'Your punishment was too severe,' said Dorcas.

'I should never have been hung!' Leakey shouted at the top of his voice.

Dorcas nodded her head.

'And my body was drained of every last drop of blood.'

'I wonder what Snail does with the blood?' Claudia whispered into Hugo's ear.

'I wish I knew,' replied Hugo.

'Your nightmare is about to end,' Dorcas promised Leakey.

'Huh! What can you do for me? No-one has the power to change the past.'

'We can release you from your punishment. Together we are strong. Together we will use this power to undo what was never meant to be.'

The crowd cheered.

'Leakey!' yelled Dorcas. 'Are you ready to strike

your soul from the book of death?'

'I-I think so,' stammered Leakey, his face distorted with worry.

'Escape death?' Claudia asked Hugo. She had thought Dorcas would be releasing him from his torment to die in peace, not to come back to life. But Hugo didn't reply, he didn't seem to hear her.

Dorcas raised her arm and shouted, 'It is time to return to the mortal world!'

Claudia watched, astonished, as Leakey stumbled back against the castle wall and fell to the ground. He looked wildly at the crowd and then let out an almighty cry. His whole body shook like a rag doll. He staggered to his feet, wheezing and clutching his chest. His heart beat loud and fast, pumping new blood through his veins. The black shadow that blighted his body melted away. Then his skin glowed and his green eyes became fresh and bright.

'I don't believe it,' said Claudia. She was thinking that if she couldn't help Daisy, maybe the spirit walk could. 'Leakey has his life back.'

'What did you do to me?' Leakey asked, taking an enormous gulp of a breath.

'Restored your dreams,' replied Dorcas. 'Take your family and return to your roots in Scotland. But remember, if you are seen in Pencliff you will be sent to the gallows for a second time, and this magic won't work twice on the same body.'

Leakey nodded gratefully. 'I've learnt my lesson.'

Scraggy stepped forward, waving an arm in the air. Suddenly, the purple puffin appeared – the exact same one as Claudia had seen on her windowsill! She watched, holding her breath, as the bird swooped down and landed on the castle wall. The puffin's eyes lit the steep stone steps that led to the shore.

'Is that Dorcas's purple puffin?' whispered Claudia.

'The one and only Padwick,' said Hugo.

'Interesting.' Claudia realised that Dorcas's puffin must have somehow made it through to her time. Did that mean that it had been Dorcas who had sent her the key? Or was it Jasper? Or someone else?

'Thanks for everything!' cried Leakey happily.

The crowd whistled, cheered, and shouted goodbye to Leakey.

'I feel tired,' said Claudia, stumbling slightly into Hugo.

'Hold on,' Hugo said, taking her arm, 'we won't be much longer.'

Dorcas turned on her heels and hurried towards South Beach.

'What now?' said Claudia. She really did feel like she needed to rest. But she didn't want to let Dorcas down.

'Dorcas is hoping to raise enough energy to transmogrify the cytoplasmic hybrids back to humans.' Hugo was using those strange words again, but at least Claudia had some idea of what he meant this time.

She looked at the sky and blinked in disbelief as the moon changed direction. Claudia watched as it moved closer to the earth and generated a storm. The wind raged, the sea changed direction, and towering waves crashed against the jagged coastline.

Dorcas faced St Agatha's Island and lifted up her arms. She was drawing on the crowd's strength. 'Release the prisoner's from the sea jail!'

Claudia stepped forward, struggling to keep her eyes open. Suddenly, a string of firecrackers magically appeared on the beach, igniting one after another and shooting sand crabs into the air. They landed and swiftly scuttled together, swelling in size, to form larger crabs. Claudia gasped, staring at the crabs as they scurried into the sea. They paddled their legs as fast as they could towards St Agatha's Island until they

91

reached the enormous iron gate. The crabs used their claws to cut the door open to the sea jail.

'I'm confused,' said Claudia. This was completely different from what had just happened to Leakey.

'This is something that we've all been waiting for,' replied Hugo, his voice high-pitched with excitement.

Claudia stared at the island. The colossal crabs waded through the cold water, towards the prisoners. As they spotted the crabs, the captives panicked and swam to the other side of the cave, and scrambled up the side of the rocks. The prisoner's slimy tails dangled in the deep water. The ravenous crabs sank their pincers into the prisoners' tails, tore at the flesh that trapped their legs together, and shoved the tissue into their mouths.

'Help!' screamed prisoners as the crabs approached them. 'Someone, please help us.'

'Do not fear!' Dorcas's voice echoed into the cave and back. 'The crabs will not harm you.'

'What are they doing?' asked Claudia, almost unable to look at the gory scene.

'Chewing the tails off – but don't worry. The townsfolk won't come to any harm.'

Claudia breathed a sigh of relief and turned back to the cave. The prisoners broke free, unharmed by the crabs. They wriggled and kicked their blood-soaked legs in the cold water. Then they climbed onto the rocks, bedraggled and wrapped rags around their bodies.

Dorcas watched the moon as the storm gradually subsided. The sea calmed.

'Look!' cried Hugo, breaking into a huge smile. 'They're human again.'

Claudia gazed at the mouth of the cave. She could see the freed prisoners bobbing up and down on the swell after they'd jumped back into the water to swim to the mainland. They clearly understood that the crabs were there to help, and some were able to hitch a ride back to the beach.

The crowd clapped and cheered and slapped each other on the back. Then they made their way down the stone steps and ran across the sand. As the prisoners emerged on the shore, the townsfolk rushed forward, taking off coats, and sweaters, and boots, and anything that could cover the prisoners' shivering bodies. Friends and families were reunited, and they hugged and kissed each other.

'You have your lives back,' shouted Dorcas, waving from the cliff.

The next moment, the crabs walked sideways out of the sea, across the beach, and then came to an abrupt standstill. There they shrank back to their normal size before burrowing into the sand and disappearing.

'Once my uncle hears about this, he'll be furious with Dorcas,' said Hugo. 'I wonder what she'll tell him.'

Claudia felt the blood drain from her face and she almost collapsed into Hugo's arms.

'Are you alright?' he asked, holding her steady.

'I'm exhausted,' moaned Claudia as the last remaining drop of strength left her body.

'It's over now,' said Hugo. 'You'll be alright in a minute.'

Claudia felt dizzy. She stumbled towards Hugo, passed out from exhaustion, and collapsed into his arms.

19

LADY PUCKETT'S PARTY

'Claudia, are you alright?' Hugo hauled her to her feet, holding her up by one arm when she wobbled.

'Err… yes… I think so,' Claudia croaked. 'I'm so sorry, I don't know what happened.'

'Can you make it back?'

Claudia took a deep, steadying breath. 'Of course.'

'Let's go then.'

When Claudia and Hugo arrived back at the Tudor Merchant's House, a light sprinkling of rain and a cool breeze blew from the sea. They leant against the hefty oak door and warmed themselves on the oil lamp swinging above their heads.

Dorcas lifted her hood.

'Thank you for your support,' she said, hurrying along the alleyway that led to Lower Puffin Place.

'Why am I so tired?' Claudia was trying to pull herself together.

'Dorcas drew on your inner strength,' explained Hugo. 'The rest of us are used to it.'

Claudia's heart dropped into the pit of her stomach. 'Really?' she said, rubbing her eyes and stifling a yawn.

'We'd better get back to the house, now.' She was desperate to speak to Daisy at the party.

'You don't have to stay late at the party if you're tired,' Hugo assured her.

Claudia nodded.

Hugo held Claudia's arm as they made their way carefully back to Upper Puffin Place. As they approached the house, they were confronted by the rumble of horse-drawn carriages on the road. Guests were flocking to the party.

'I'm feeling a bit better now,' said Claudia, breaking free from Hugo's grip.

'Oh dear - we're late,' he replied, red-faced. 'We'll be in trouble.'

They slipped past Arnold who was greeting some people at the front door and rushed into the hallway.

'Where have you been?' said a maid. 'Arnold has sent Daisy out to look for you.'

'Sorry, Violet,' said Hugo. 'I lost track of the time.'

'Can I speak to Daisy when she gets back?' asked Claudia, wishing she had spoken to her when she'd had the chance.

'What about?' asked Hugo.

'It's not important,' fibbed Claudia, wondering how much she could confide in him. He'd never believe that she was from a different time. 'Maybe I can catch her later.'

'Yes,' said Hugo.

'Good evening, Your Honour,' came Arnold's voice behind them. 'I hope you and Lady Agatha are well.'

'It's Uncle Septimus,' Hugo said to Claudia.

She spun round.

'I think he's coming over to speak to us,' said Hugo as Snail strode in their direction.

'Sorry I was in such a hurry today,' said Septimus, apologetically. 'I really couldn't stop to talk. What have you two been doing?'

'Nothing,' denied Hugo. 'We've been busy helping with the party, haven't we, Claudia?'

Claudia bit her lower lip and nodded.

'Oh, well then, you've still got a lot of work to do. The celebrations have only just begun. I'll see you both later.' Septimus took Lady Agatha's arm and joined the party. As Hugo and Claudia followed him into the drawing room, Claudia noticed people swiftly moving away to avoid eye contact with him, while others stood up and quickly took to the dance floor.

'I wonder what's keeping my parents,' Hugo said, glancing around. 'I'm looking forward to introducing you to them.'

Claudia smiled.

'Come on,' said Hugo. 'Let's enjoy ourselves.'

'Great idea,' agreed Claudia, although she really wasn't bothered about enjoying it. All she could think about now was finding Daisy. But she'd been sent out of the house to find Claudia and Hugo. *I'll just have to wait until she gives up searching for us, and comes back to the house.*

The room shimmered in the candlelight, lighting the faces of people with grand titles. Hugo introduced various Baronesses and Earls and Lords and Ladys to Claudia as they moved around, all of whose names were immediately forgotten. The soft sound of a piano could be heard in the background, playing the most romantic music Claudia had ever heard. Couples swirled and twirled around the room in their elegant, pastel-coloured gowns and tailored suits.

'Excuse me,' said a waiter holding a silver tray laden with crystal glasses and canapés, 'would you like something?'

'No thanks,' replied Claudia, shuffling to one side to let the waiter pass as she scanned the room for Daisy.

Lady Puckett was seated in the centre of the room. She was surrounded by ladies wishing her well and presenting her with exquisitely wrapped gifts.

'Here they are,' Hugo said, smiling and pointing

at the door. A noble-looking pair entered the room.

'I present Lord and Lady Hamilton-Barnes,' Arnold announced loudly to the room.

A wave of warm applause caused Claudia to swing towards the door, and her eyes lit up. Hugo's mother stole the limelight in a beautiful lilac gown that glittered with gemstones. Her husband was a fair-haired, handsome man, tall in stature and distinguished in appearance. They glided around the room, graciously greeting their guests.

Claudia followed Hugo across the room, but before Hugo had a chance to approach his father, Snail stepped in front of him with his wife at his side.

'Good evening, Henry,' said Septimus.

'Septimus. Agatha.' Hugo's father nodded. 'How are you both?'

'We're very well, thank you,' replied Septimus. 'I think you would agree that I've got the town running quite smoothly at present.'

He raised one eyebrow and said, 'I suppose so.'

Agatha stepped forward to greet her sister. 'It's lovely to see you, Lucinda.'

'I'm delighted that you could join us,' said Hugo's mother, kissing her on the cheek.

'Where's Hugo?' asked Agatha.

'I'm here,' said Hugo as he appeared with Claudia at his side.

'Hello, Aunt Agatha,' said Hugo. 'Please meet Claudia. She's visiting us for a short while.'

'What a charming girl.' Agatha's face lit up as she asked, 'Wherever did she come from?'

Claudia felt a moment of panic. 'Not far from here,' she lied. She dared not mention Jasper and Daisy.

'Well you must come and show your face at Chillingbone Castle before you leave,' suggested Agatha. 'It's a fascinating place, and I'm sure Hugo will enjoy showing you around, especially the dungeons.'

Septimus smiled. 'You're welcome any time.'

Hugo gestured to his parents. 'This is Lord Henry and Lady Lucinda, Claudia.'

'It's so nice to meet you, Claudia,' said Henry, nodding politely. 'Hugo could do with some company.'

'Yes,' said Lucinda, breaking into a wide smile. 'Stay as long as you like.'

Claudia's face lit up. She was pleased with the warm welcome and it made her wonder if perhaps Hugo was as lonely as she was.

'I think you would agree, Henry, that I've got the town running very smoothly at the moment,' repeated Septimus, smirking.

'As long as you're happy,' Henry grunted. 'I hear that you've been investing in precious stones.'

'It's a really good investment,' said Septimus. 'We ought to get together some time and do some business.'

'I'm afraid I'm far too busy for that,' muttered Henry in a light, dismissive tone. 'I have more than enough work to do already.'

'You must have some spare time,' said Septimus. 'We could control the diamond market together.'

'It's not for me,' Henry said firmly.

Claudia noticed that Henry's hands were trembling slightly. He had clamped them together behind his back in an attempt to look relaxed. She wondered what he really thought of his brother-in-law.

'Very well,' said Septimus. 'Let me know if you change your mind.'

Claudia stepped back and glanced around the room, trying to catch sight of Daisy.

'Are you looking for someone?' asked Hugo.

'I was just wondering if Daisy was back yet?'

98

Hugo checked his watch. 'Daisy will be upstairs now. She'll stay in Lady Puckett's quarters all night, waiting to attend to her after the party.'

There was little point in her hanging around down here then, especially not at a boring adults' party. 'I hope you don't mind, but I think I'll be off to bed,' she said, yawning. 'I know the way.'

'Not at all,' replied Hugo. 'Thank you again for your help tonight.'

'Good night everyone,' said Claudia, leaving the party. Her mind was buzzing and her body was exhausted, after the walk with Dorcas. She pretended to go upstairs to bed, but instead slipped into the grandfather clock in the hall when no-one was looking.

When the door slammed behind her, the clock shuddered as though in an earthquake. She was used to the travel through time now, so she braced herself. She was annoyed that she hadn't had a chance to talk to Daisy. Once the clock stopped, the door opened and the pendulum moved aside for her to leave. She breathed a sigh of relief and jumped out. Then she headed along the dimly lit corridor and ran into her room. Instantly, the great white house, with its glittering lights, diminished in size. The lights flashed off and it fell into darkness.

It's still eight o'clock in the morning here. Mum will be coming up for me soon. I must remember what I was doing when I go back to Pencliff. She climbed wearily into bed and crawled under the duvet. As she closed her eyes, she heard a knock on the door. 'Morning, darling,' said her mother, coming in. 'What can I get you for breakfast?'

'I'm not feeling very well,' replied Claudia, holding her head and moaning. 'Is it OK if I stay in bed today?' She wanted to get back to Pencliff, but first she had to get some sleep. She would never be able to help Daisy feeling this tired.

'Of course,' said her mother, frowning. 'You do look rather pale. Call me if you need anything.'

20

MURDER AND THIEVERY

'Who's there?' groaned Claudia sleepily, as Sekora gently pawed her face. She rolled over and sat up in bed, confused and disorientated.

Switching on her bedside lamp, she gasped. There was blood everywhere. It was smeared over the bed sheets and trailed along the floor. Sitting up straighter, Claudia saw blood on Sekora's paws. She reeled and she blinked in disbelief.

'What's happening?' Her voice trembled.

Claudia looked down, trying to stay calm, and noticed that there were bloody paw prints coming from the doll's house.

'Whose blood could this be?'

She glanced at the clock. It was two in the morning. She climbed out of bed, feeling sick to her stomach, aware that something terrible had happened. 'Let's get back to the house.' She slumped onto the floor, facing the doll's house. She placed Sekora on her lap, and pushed the front door open. Suddenly, the lights in the hallway glistened like tiny diamonds and the house grew out of the floor like a giant, inflatable toy.

Sekora jumped out of Claudia's arms and scampered through the door. Claudia took a deep breath and ran into the house, along the corridor, following the trail of blood. Her legs felt like lead, but she kept running until she spotted Sekora, meowing outside the clock. As Claudia set the hands to two o'clock, a brightly lit full moon advanced across the dial, the calm seascape became a violent storm, and the waves carried off the planets. As the door clicked open, the chimes echoed eerily in her ears and she scuttled past the pendulum, followed by her cat.

This journey through time made her feel sick. As she stepped out in Pencliff, she was disoriented and almost tripped up over Sekora. She glanced around. Even though the house was in darkness several members of staff were rushing in and out of the rooms. A bolt of lightning flashed across the night sky, briefly lighting up the hallway. Sekora whined, hiding behind Claudia's legs.

'What's happening?' Claudia asked a servant.

'The Mistress has found a dead body,' he replied, shaking violently. 'The Master has called the police.'

Sekora yowled, as though in pain.

'Dead! Who's dead?' Claudia felt her insides go cold. She remembered how Sekora had reacted on the train, and she wondered if he linked storms to death. The servant didn't answer. He just disappeared through a door.

As Claudia headed along the hallway, her whole body started to tremble. *What if it's Hugo?* She hated the thought of losing her new friend.

'There you are!' said a loud voice from behind her.

Claudia spun around and gasped. 'You're alive!' Then she sighed heavily. 'I thought you'd been murdered.'

'No, it's Violet,' said Hugo, frowning.

'Oh no!' gasped Claudia, feeling bad that it had happened when she wasn't around.

'I overheard the servants saying that she was stabbed in the back, in my mother's dressing room,' explained Hugo, 'while she was locking away the ballgown she wore to the party.'

'Stabbed!' Claudia's heart beat faster. She remembered the tiny bloody knife that she'd found in the doll's house on Christmas day. 'What did your parents say?

'I don't know.' Hugo shrugged. 'I haven't spoken to them yet. But I think my father is in the library, waiting for the police. Let's go and have a word with him.'

Without even needing to discuss it, they headed towards the library at the back of the house. Behind them, the front door banged shut. They turned around to see two policemen taking off their hats and wiping their feet on the rug in the hall.

'Inspector Squibbs and Constable Horrod, Lord Henry is expecting you,' said Arnold, showing the officers into the library. He opened the door and announced their arrival.

'Thank you, Arnold,' said Lord Henry. 'That will be all.'

'As you wish, my Lord.' Closing the door, Arnold disappeared downstairs to the servant's quarters.

Claudia and Hugo shuffled together to the door and pressed their ears against it.

'Thank you for coming, Inspector,' replied Lord Henry. 'I'm absolutely shocked and deeply saddened by what has happened to poor Violet. We will all miss her very much.'

'Nasty business,' said Squibbs. 'The body will be removed as soon as possible.'

'I'm very grateful,' Lord Henry said. 'I'll be visiting Violet's family later today.'

'Do you know if Violet had any enemies?' asked Squibbs.

'None whatsoever, as far as I'm aware,' sighed Lord Henry. 'She was a sweet girl, and a popular member of the household.'

'Has anything gone missing?'

'Quite a lot of jewellery, including my wife's priceless purple diamond.'

'I'm sorry to hear that,' said Squibbs. 'Perhaps your wife could provide us with a detailed description of every item that has been taken?'

'Certainly,' replied Lord Henry. 'Of course you can't compare the value of the jewellery to that of Violet's life.'

'Were any of the guests in the house at the time of the murder?' asked Squibbs.

'My brother-in-law, Sir Septimus Snail, and his wife were the last to leave the party and we waved them off at around midnight.' Lord Henry shook his head. 'Violet was definitely still alive then. She brought my wife a hot drink before bed and took her gown to the dressing room.'

'I'll need a room to interview all the staff,' said Squibbs. 'We have to know exactly where they all were at the time of the murder.'

'Of course. There was one other person I'd forgotten about. Hugo has a friend staying at the moment.'

Squibbs grunted. 'I'll make a note of that.'

Claudia's jaw dropped. What if she became a suspect?

'The small study is yours for as long as you need it,' offered Lord Henry.

'Much appreciated,' said Squibbs. 'We'll try not to cause too much disruption to you or your family.'

'Well thank you, Inspector,' said Lord Henry. 'I have every confidence that you'll find the murderer and retrieve the jewellery.'

Claudia heard footsteps. 'Someone's coming,' she said, nudging Hugo, and they stepped back from the door. Squibbs strode into the hall and spotted Hugo and Claudia heading off in the opposite direction. 'I need to have a word with you both.'

Hugo stopped and turned around, smiling sweetly. 'Certainly, Inspector,' he said.

Squibbs took out his notebook, and said, 'I need to know your whereabouts last night.'

'Claudia and I were at the party,' said Hugo, 'and then I walked Claudia to her bedroom at around eleven thirty. We were both fast asleep at the time Violet was murdered.'

Squibbs stared at Claudia. 'Is that right?'

'Y-yes,' she stuttered. It wasn't exactly true, but grateful that Hugo had supplied her with an alibi.

Squibbs scribbled in his notebook. 'Right, Horrod, round up the staff.'

'Yes, sir.'

Hugo and Claudia ran off to the sofa at the other end of the hall.

'I wonder who murdered Violet,' sighed Hugo.

'Maybe someone broke into the house while we were at the party,' Claudia said.

'You're probably right.' Hugo nodded. 'But why would anyone want to kill poor Violet?'

'I don't know. Maybe she caught them trying to rob your parents or something. It's something that we'll need to find out.'

'My mother is terribly upset. She always liked her.'

'Your father said that some jewellery was missing?'

'She won't be too bothered about that... apart from...'

'What is it, Hugo? You know you can trust me.'

'I know I can.' Hugo nodded and smiled. 'Her purple diamond's disappeared. It probably fell out of her dress during the party. That is, unless someone popped it out without her noticing.'

'Is it very valuable?'

'It's the most valuable diamond in the world,' he explained, 'and it has a long and mysterious past.

That's why my mother hid it amongst the other jewels in her dress. She hoped that people would think it was a costume jewel. A fake.'

Claudia imagined Lady Lucinda dancing around the drawing room. Few people would know that her dress hid a secret in plain sight. 'What's mysterious about it?'

'My mother hasn't told me everything,' said Hugo, lowering his voice even further. None of the adults seemed to care that they were around, but Claudia understood that he would want to be careful about what he said, under the circumstances.

'Although I do know that it's a wish-fulfilling jewel that could be dangerous if it fell into the wrong hands.'

Claudia stared at him with a stony face. After all she had experienced in Pencliff, she didn't doubt Hugo's explanation.

'Once the jewel is removed from the claw setting, the diamond's power will be diminished,' confided Hugo. 'But it still remains a beautiful and priceless stone that is very desirable.'

Claudia shook her head, feeling sick with worry. After listening to the discussions between Squibbs and Lord Henry, she didn't have a clue who could have committed the murder, or stolen the diamond. Everyone had apparently left the house when it went missing and the murder occurred.

This had to be what Daisy was blamed for - the robbery and the murder. But how was Claudia going to clear her name? She was furious at herself for not speaking to Daisy last time she'd been here.

'We'd better try to get some sleep,' suggested Hugo. 'There's nothing we can do right now.'

'I'll see you in the morning,' she nodded, although she had no intention of going to bed. She'd had an idea, and she needed to get back home right away.

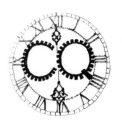

21

FINGERPRINTING

'Damn!' Claudia stared at her bedside clock and sighed heavily. She wished it wasn't still two o'clock in the morning as she needed to speak to her dad but couldn't wake him up in the middle of the night. Collapsing into her comfy chair, she realised the only thing to do would be to wait for her parents to wake up.

Time crawled slowly. She tried to calm her nerves, but all she could think about was Daisy. Finally her eyes started to close and she dozed off into a restless sleep.

'Daisy's innocent,' she mumbled, dreaming of her on the gallows. 'Leave her alone. She's done nothing wrong. Please... she didn't do it. Trust me... I just need a few more days to prove it.' Her dreams were filled with blood and jewels, and a terrifying stranger standing in the shadows, holding a knife.

'Morning, darling.' Her dad's voice interrupted her dream, and Claudia flashed her eyes open. He came into the room with a big smile on his face. 'Would you like some breakfast?'

'Not at the moment,' replied Claudia, 'but I do need some help with a problem I've got.'

Her dad strode across the room and pulled open the curtains. 'It's a bit early for problems, but I'll see what I can do.'

'I'm working on a biology project on fingerprints,'

Claudia explained. 'But I don't know anything about it. When was it first introduced?'

Her father's face lit up. Claudia knew this was the kind of problem he liked, something law-based. 'The first fingerprint evidence for identification purposes was in England in 1902. It wasn't accepted at first, but it soon became a powerful tool in the fight against crime.'

That's after the date on the newspaper cutting Jasper sent me. If they didn't have fingerprinting then, it couldn't prove Daisy was innocent. But what if I bring it back in time a little?

'We have a book on it in my study.' Her father disappeared out of the door. 'I'll be back shortly.'

'OK, Dad, Thanks.'

Claudia's father returned with a big brown book. 'Here it is,' he said. '*Classification and Uses of Fingerprints.*'

'That's brilliant.' Claudia rushed towards her father and grabbed the heavy volume out of his hands. 'I'll read this.'

'I'll leave you in peace then. Good luck with the project.'

Claudia searched through the book, frantically flicking through the pages to find the right page. At last she found what she was looking for. She ripped it out and stuffed it into her pocket, then jumped onto a chair and lifted down her chemistry set. She threw the lid on the floor and her eyes scanned the labels of the glass phials. *Lethal Leeches... Devil's Denial... Violent Blood... Curious Chlorine.* Aha! *Aluminium powder for fine fast finger-printing.*'

She checked the time: it was half-past nine so she swiftly bundled the phial, a brush, and some sticky tape into her tote bag. Then she turned to the doll's house and pushed open the front door. The house creaked and groaned and grew as before, rising into the air. She ran inside, to the end of the shadowy hallway, with her bag over her shoulder, and quickly set the silver hands.

Once again, she held on tight as the marvellous magical mechanism chimed and ticked and rocked its way through time.

Claudia flew out through the door, running towards the staircase, desperate to speak to Hugo about fingerprinting. Her mind was racing with excitement. As she got nearer, however, she stopped in her tracks, surprised to hear a terrible commotion going on downstairs in the servants' quarters. Squibbs and Horrod appeared in the hallway, holding Daisy in handcuffs.

'Please, believe me!' Daisy was sobbing and crying. 'I'm innocent. I was nowhere near the dressing room... Violet was my friend!'

'It's no good denying it,' said Squibbs, stern-faced. 'We've got all the evidence we need.'

At that moment, Hugo dashed downstairs, and Claudia grabbed his arm.

'Daisy wouldn't hurt a fly!' gasped Claudia.

'Of course she wouldn't,' said Hugo reassuringly. 'I'll speak to my father.'

'Can you do it quickly?' pleaded Claudia. 'Looks like Squibbs means business.'

Hugo and Claudia burst into the sitting room.

'Why have the police arrested Daisy?' asked Hugo unhappily. 'She's not capable of murder!'

Is it really too late? She hated the idea of Daisy being hung for a crime she didn't commit – and of letting down Jasper.

Lord Henry lowered his newspaper. He stood up and moved slowly across the room. 'After conducting a thorough investigation of the facts, and interviewing all the staff, Inspector Squibbs has concluded that Daisy was the last person to see Violet alive.'

'But what evidence do they have?' asked Hugo, nostrils flaring.

'She was seen by one of the staff leaving the dressing room at the time that the crime was committed,' his father replied.

Claudia stepped back, flattening herself against the wall. She bit her lip. There were questions that she wanted to ask him, but she was afraid of saying the wrong thing.

'Who saw her?' exclaimed Hugo.

Lord Henry raised his eyebrows. 'There's more. The police discovered a blood-stained knife in Daisy's bedroom.'

'I don't believe a word of it. Daisy and Violet were good friends,' protested Hugo. 'Did they find any jewellery in Daisy's room?'

'No, but she could have gotten rid of it!' snapped Lord Henry. 'Hugo, I don't want you getting involved in this matter. That's my last word on the subject.'

'Alright, Father,' sighed Hugo. He beckoned Claudia over. She knew it was time to leave.

'We've got to do something!' said Claudia as they left the room.

'I wonder who planted the knife?'

'The murderer, of course,' whispered Claudia, trembling and looking around. 'It has to be.'

'I was thinking the same. Let's see if Dorcas knows anything,' suggested Hugo, as they headed through the front door. 'She always knows what to do.'

Claudia nodded. She realised it might be better to wait and see what Dorcas had to say before she suggested fingerprinting. Trying to give her mind some time to settle, she asked, 'Was there much trouble in the town last night with the prankster spirits?'

'I didn't hear about any trouble, thank goodness.'

By the time they'd sprinted to the end of Upper

Puffin Place, Claudia and Hugo were both out of breath. They slumped against a wall, breathing deeply for a moment, and then they continued running.

'What's that sickly smell?' panted Claudia, as she sniffed the air. 'Is someone burning bats?'

'Some of the townsfolk cook puffin pie,' sighed Hugo. 'They even shoot the birds because they believe they're a nuisance and that they deprive the town of fresh fish.'

'That's rubbish,' snapped Claudia. 'They don't eat that much fish, do they? And they're beautiful creatures. They aren't a nuisance!'

'There are people in Pencliff who are determined to hunt the birds to extinction.' Hugo pulled a handkerchief from his pocket and wiped his sweaty forehead. 'They're jealous of their relationship with Dorcas.'

'Here we are,' said Claudia, spotting the puffin door-knocker. She was desperate to speak to Dorcas, but wondered what the sorceress could do. According to the police, they had all the evidence they needed to convict Daisy.

Hugo burst through the front door, with Claudia right behind him.

'I've been expecting you,' said Dorcas. She was sitting next to the fireplace, wearing a flowing lilac dress that matched the colour of her eyes. Sekora was on her lap, purring contentedly as she tickled him under his chin. He meowed with delight, jumped down, and affectionately rubbed his body against Claudia's leg.

'I wondered where you were,' said Claudia, smiling briefly at her cat. She crouched down to stroke him.

'Take a seat,' said Dorcas, gesturing to the armchairs next to her.

'Daisy's been arrested for murder,' blurted out

Hugo, as he collapsed into a comfy chair.'

'I know, Scraggy told me,' replied Dorcas. 'The whole thing is ridiculous. Daisy wouldn't harm a soul, or steal your mother's jewellery.'

Hugo sighed heavily. 'Do you think that the killer is the same person that has the jewellery?'

'I think so,' said Dorcas. 'Maybe Violet disturbed the murderer in the dressing room and he had to kill her.'

'That's what we thought. The problem is that the police found the knife that killed Violet in Daisy's room,' explained Hugo.

Dorcas shook her head sadly. 'I'm guessing it was planted by the real killer. Or maybe someone who works there was paid to plant it in her room.'

'You're right,' replied Claudia. 'We tried talking to Hugo's dad but he doesn't want us to get involved.'

'Mark my words,' said Dorcas, shaking her head again. 'The culprit will hang by a thick rope. Cousin Septimus doesn't pull any punches when it comes to punishing crimes like this.'

'More so in this case, since my uncle doesn't like anyone messing with his family,' added Hugo. 'He's always been very fond of my mother.'

Claudia's mind was racing. Catching the real criminal didn't matter if Daisy was framed.

She suddenly remembered the conversation she'd overheard between Foggy and Jack, and wondered whether they were involved in some way. She had been convinced that they were up to no good. But how would she find them? And even if she did, the police would never believe her.

'It's going to be hard to track down a cold-blooded killer,' Dorcas said as she stoked the fire. 'He'll know how to cover his tracks and destroy damning evidence that would tie him to a crime. Anyone who tries to frame someone else for a murder has obviously given the crime some thought.'

'It's true,' Hugo agreed. 'There are a lot of shadowy characters in Pencliff. The murderer may have already smuggled the jewellery out of the country and left.'

'Really? But then we'll never be able to prove Daisy's innocent!' Claudia felt sick with worry.

'Somehow I don't think that the murderer would leave town straight away, Hugo,' said Dorcas. 'He's probably carrying on as normal. It would attract attention if someone left unexpectedly.'

'But what can we do?' asked Claudia, pulling at her hair in frustration. 'Hugo's dad has warned us not to get involved.'

'Someone at the house must have seen something,' Dorcas urged. 'But you must be quick. Scraggy has heard that Daisy is set to be tried and convicted of murder tomorrow.'

Claudia's stomach churned.

'We'd better get going,' she said, jumping up. 'We've got to set a trap for the real killer.'

'Be very careful,' warned Dorcas. 'If the murderer finds out that you're after him, he might try to silence you too. Remember, he's not afraid to kill.'

22

THE KEY

'I've got a plan,' whispered Claudia as they entered the big house.

'I'm parched,' Hugo said. 'Do you mind if we discuss it over a cup of tea?'

'OK,' agreed Claudia. She didn't think they had time for a drink, but didn't want to be rude.

'Good day, Master Hugo,' said Arnold. 'Can I get you children anything?'

'That would be nice,' Hugo nodded. 'Could we have some tea and sandwiches in the dining room, please?'

'Certainly. I won't be a moment.' Slipping out, Arnold made his way downstairs to the kitchen.

Hugo opened the double doors for Claudia and they took a seat at the table. Claudia pulled out the page on fingerprinting from her pocket and handed it to Hugo. 'I think I know how we can catch Violet's murderer.'

Hugo took the page and sat in silence, reading the article. 'Fingerprinting? Where on earth did you get this?'

'It's a new invention,' Claudia said quickly. 'Squibbs knows nothing about it, so it's up to us to collect the evidence and trap the murderer.'

'It's amazing,' Hugo mumbled under his breath.

'I think it'll prove Daisy is innocent,' said Claudia,

smiling, 'and that her fingerprints are not on the knife.'

'I hope the murderer wasn't wearing gloves,' replied Hugo, 'or we've had it. It's like Dorcas said: someone must have seen something.'

'You're right, we can keep asking questions. Maybe one of the staff can remember seeing Daisy at the time of the murder.'

The door opened and Arnold walked in carrying a silver tray with a china teapot, a jug of hot water, cutlery and crockery, and salmon and cream cheese sandwiches cut into triangles.

'Thank you, Arnold,' said Hugo, swiftly handing back Claudia the page. She stuffed it into her pocket.

'Reading something interesting?' asked Arnold, as he laid out the cups and started serving the tea.

'Err…' said Claudia, pulling the cup towards her, 'it's to do with Daisy.'

Arnold moved closer. 'What is it?'

'It's just an article about solving crimes,' said Claudia, realising that this was a chance to pick his brain. 'You must be upset that Daisy has been accused of murdering Violet.'

Arnold nodded. 'I am, but I don't interfere in police matters and neither should you or Hugo. Lord Henry wouldn't like it.'

'We're only trying to help,' muttered Claudia.

Hugo offered Claudia a sandwich and then he helped himself. She took a bite of her sandwich. 'You do make particularly good sandwiches.'

'Thank you,' Arnold brightened.

'Perhaps,' urged Claudia, 'you can remember seeing Daisy on the night of the murder, and can vouch for the fact that she was nowhere near Lady Lucinda's dressing room.'

'That's not what I saw,' said Arnold in a stern voice. 'And I've already given my statement to the police. I can't change it now.'

'I-I wasn't suggesting that you make something up,' stuttered Claudia, feeling her cheeks flush. 'I just thought that you might have remembered where she was when the murder was committed.'

'I was rushed off my feet,' Arnold said. 'I was busy looking after the guests and making sure that Lady Puckett had everything she needed.'

'Did you know that the police didn't find any of the missing jewellery when they searched Daisy's room?' said Claudia. 'And she wouldn't have had time to sell it.'

'I'm sorry I can't be more helpful.'

'Maybe someone entered the house by the servant's quarters when they were all busy serving the guests,' suggested Claudia. 'They could have slipped upstairs when no-one was looking and waited until the party was over.'

'Wait, Claudia. That can't be right,' interrupted Hugo, leaning over to take another sandwich. 'Don't you remember that my father said Daisy was seen leaving my mother's dressing room at the time Violet was murdered?'

'I wonder who told the police that. Do you know?' Claudia asked Arnold, catching his eye.

Arnold sighed disapprovingly. 'Unfortunately, I have no idea.'

'Is Daisy still at the police station?' Hugo asked.

'Your father will probably know what's happening,' replied Arnold. 'Is there anything else that I can get you?'

'I don't think so.' Hugo stood up and moved towards the door. 'We'll see you later.'

'Sorry, Hugo. I know I went on a bit at Arnold,' whispered Claudia, once they'd left the room. 'He seemed a bit agitated. I hope I didn't upset him.'

'Don't worry,' said Hugo. 'My father probably asked Arnold not to discuss the matter with anyone.

He wouldn't agree with us meddling in police business.'

When Claudia opened her bedroom door she tried to act naturally, as though she had been in there before. It was a perfectly square room painted green, with a large window overlooking the front garden. There was a highly polished brass bed in the centre of the room, rich red mahogany furniture, and a walk-in wardrobe.

'What's the plan?' asked Hugo.

Claudia put her hands on her hips. 'There's only one thing for it; we need a list of all the staff who hold a set of keys.'

'You're right.' Hugo nodded. 'But first we need to borrow my mother's key for the dressing room to collect some fingerprints.'

'Let's get going,' said Claudia eagerly.

'Follow me.' Hugo opened the door and they hurried out of the room and along the corridor to his mother's bedroom door. He knocked. There was no answer, so they slipped inside. Claudia immediately recognised the room and the oil painting on the wall of Lady Lucinda. This was the room where she had hidden in the wardrobe, listening to Daisy and Violet.

'I won't be a moment,' said Hugo, as he hurried across the room. He picked up a casket off the dressing table, pushed a silver knob on its side, and a secret drawer, lined with red velvet, flew open.

Claudia pinned her ear to the door.

'Got it!' said Hugo, lifting out a brass key.

'There's someone coming,' warned Claudia, as she crept back from the door.

Hugo and Claudia both froze, fixing their gaze on each other. Claudia held her breath as she heard heavy footsteps in the corridor outside getting louder. There was a click and the door opened.

23

THE DRESSING ROOM

Hugo gestured Claudia to follow. They tiptoed towards the four-poster bed, crouched down, and were just about to crawl underneath when the door suddenly slammed shut and the footsteps faded away. They stood up and both exhaled a long breath at the same time.

'That was close,' Claudia sighed. 'They must have changed their mind.'

Hugo held out the key and said, 'Can you collect the fingerprints? And I'll try to find out how many servants hold keys.'

'Good idea!' As Claudia took the key, the purple puffin flashed through her mind and she remembered the snowflake turning into a key.

'You need to be quick, as the servants are always in and out of the dressing room,' warned Hugo, as he opened the door and peeped around. 'Be careful. Someone may be watching us.' He headed in the opposite direction and down the stairs.

Claudia crept out of the bedroom and along the landing, until she was close to the dressing room door. Her eyes darted around to make sure no-one had seen her. She quickly jammed the key into the lock and it turned with some difficulty. She pushed open the door and hurried into a big, gloomy room. There were flickering candles on a low chest, casting distorted shadows on the wall. As her eyes adjusted she caught sight of a large, old-fashioned wooden wardrobe in the far corner of the room. She paused, imagining Violet's last steps before she was murdered. Claudia pictured her entering the room, carrying the silk gown over her arm and humming a happy tune. Violet hung the gown on the wardrobe door and was buttoning up the back when a stranger crept up behind her and plunged a knife into her. Claudia lunged forward and imagined where the body would land. She shuddered in horror as she visualised Violet lying on the floor, blood oozing out of her back.

She examined the bottom of the wardrobe door, but couldn't see any fingerprints. Pulling out the powder from her bag, she dusted the door around the brass lock and stood back.

There's nothing there! She knelt down and blew lightly over the surface of each powder mark. But as she stood up, she heard footsteps outside the room and quickly hid in the wardrobe.

'Now then,' sighed a voice. 'What was it that the mistress wanted?'

'Don't ask me, Alice! I wish you'd hurry up. It gives me the creeps in here now.'

'Well it wasn't me, Charlotte,' said Alice. 'I know, she wanted her black coat. It's probably in the wardrobe.'

Claudia pushed herself to the back of the wardrobe, hiding behind a long, red gown. *What will I do? She's going to look in here! Please don't see me!*

'Is this it, Alice?'

'Yes, that's the one, Charlotte.'

Alice sighed heavily. 'Wonder who left it on the chair.'

'The mistress would be very cross if she knew,' said Charlotte. 'Now let's get out of here. This place puts me on edge.'

The bedroom door closed behind the two maids, and Claudia quietly breathed a sigh of relief. *That was too close!* She climbed out of the wardrobe and took another look at the door. She noticed a fat fingerprint, smudged with a trace of dried blood further down than she'd been looking before.

There it is!

She transferred the print onto a bit of sticky tape, stuck it to a piece of paper, popped it in her bag, and headed across the room. Then she opened the door a crack and peeked out, just as Arnold passed the room and headed towards the staircase. Claudia tiptoed through the door, quickly locked it behind her, and ran back to her bedroom.

'Find anything?' asked Hugo from inside as Claudia opened the door.

'Oh, you scared me,' she said with a jump. 'I nearly bumped into Arnold on the way out.' She screwed up her face. 'I'm sure he didn't see me.'

'I hope not,' Hugo replied. 'Arnold would go mad if he caught either of us in there, especially after what he said earlier about us not getting involved. And he'd tell my father.'

'That room makes my skin crawl, and I nearly got caught by a servant looking for your mother's coat,' said Claudia. 'But I think I've found the killer's fingerprint.'

'I should have gone with you,' sighed Hugo.

'It's OK. Anyway, how did you get on?'

'I've got the list of the servants who hold keys.'

Hugo handed it over. 'My mother wasn't very happy though. She told me that I shouldn't be poking my nose into police business.'

Claudia scanned the names. 'This could take forever.'

'May as well start straight away. I'll begin by collecting the staff's fingerprints. That's the only way we can prove that one of them is involved in the murder,' said Hugo. 'I think I should do it alone. Arnold may not like it if someone he barely knows is snooping around. He'd think we were playing a game, making light of Violet's death. Sorry, Claudia.'

'No problem. It makes sense.'

Claudia wished she had something to occupy her while she waited. She closed the door. Lounging in a plush chair, she spent the next few hours thinking about Daisy and worrying that she didn't have enough time to clear her name. She took deep breath after deep breath to steady her nerves. Whoever had murdered Violet was clearly unbalanced. *What if the killer finds out what we are up to, and comes after us?*

***

TAP! TAP!

'Come in,' said Claudia, opening her eyes and stretching. She had fallen asleep.

Hugo flew into the room. 'It was worse than I thought,' he said, shaking his head. 'Sneaking about and following the staff from room to room is harder than it sounds. I had to be really careful. But I got them all. I hope the staff don't mind!'

'If they're innocent they've nothing to worry about.'

Claudia grabbed the bundle of papers and placed them on a table next to the window.

'Each piece of paper has a name on it,' Hugo said. 'Let's make a start. We've got to nail the killer before Daisy is hung.'

Claudia picked up the first fingerprint, marked with the name 'Willie' and checked it against the one she had taken from the wardrobe door. 'This one's no good!'

There was a knock on the door.

'Come in,' shouted Hugo.

Lady Puckett entered the room. 'I've been looking everywhere for you, Hugo.'

'What can I do for you?'

Claudia looked up and smiled. 'Hello.'

'Hello, Claudia,' said Lady Puckett. 'Did you enjoy my party?'

'Yes,' Claudia replied. 'I had a great time.'

'Hugo, would you mind delivering some thank you cards for me?'

'Umm...' mumbled Hugo, 'can I go later?'

'They're rather urgent,' said Lady Puckett. 'After all that's happened, I want to thank the guests for coming. We have to put on a brave face otherwise they may not come again. Don't you agree?'

'Alright, I'll go right away,' he said reluctantly. 'See you later.'

Claudia waited for them to leave then eagerly looked back at the table and grabbed another piece of paper. *I've got to find a match or Daisy will die.*

24

THE MISSING FINGERPRINTS

At eight o'clock the grandfather clock chimed. The house was silent as rain slid down the window. The sun had melted away and darkness had fallen.

'It's hopeless!' sighed Claudia aloud, as she checked the last fingerprint. Her brain was dissolving with tiredness.

The door creaked open. 'Any luck?' Hugo entered the room carrying a tray with a freshly baked plum cake, hot rolls, and a selection of fresh fruit.

Claudia shook her head. 'Not one match!'

'Well, you did your best.' Hugo placed the tray on the table. 'What can we do now?'

'I'm not sure,' replied Claudia.

'Maybe the police will come up with something.'

'But Squibbs has closed the investigation.' Claudia pushed the prints away. 'He's locked up Daisy and thrown away the key. We have to find something to prove she's innocent!'

'Have something to eat,' said Hugo, handing her a plate. 'You must be starving, and no-one can think properly on an empty stomach.'

'Alright,' agreed Claudia, helping herself to an apple and a piece of cake. 'I think I'll triple-check each set of prints.'

'Start again?' said Hugo with concern. 'But you look exhausted.'

'I can't give up,' mumbled Claudia as she chewed the apple. 'I made a promise and I'm going to keep it! Daisy's innocent... we can't just let her die.' She suddenly realised she'd said too much. Hugo knew nothing about Jasper's letter. Luckily, he didn't pick up on what she'd said.

'I've got a few more chores to do for my grandmother,' remarked Hugo, closing the door. 'And then I think I'll have an early night.'

'OK,' Claudia realised that she was much more intent on solving the problem than he was. She glowered at the mass of fingerprints, convinced that something was wrong. Had she missed something? She didn't feel hungry any more. The nausea of worry had dulled her appetite. She threw her half-eaten apple on the plate, feeling terrible that she was going to let Daisy down. She settled back into her chair and, overcome by tiredness, she dozed off into a restless sleep.

Claudia was trapped inside a cold, gloomy prison, with rats running wild. She squinted, shaking as the sound of eerie screams echoed in her head. The smell of charred flesh filled her nostrils. She quickly made her way past a one-eyed guard who was brandishing a sizzling hot iron, and headed towards a door.

She stood on tiptoes and peered inside a cell. Daisy was sitting there, pale and weak, on a broken bed comprising of a dirty straw mattress. Daisy got up, staggered to the door, and rattled the bars, pleading for help. Claudia took her hand and shuddered; she had 'M' burned onto her palm. She tried to comfort Daisy, but a tall dark stranger with flaming eyes suddenly appeared and started growling, like a wild animal. He was dressed in black robes that covered his broad shoulders and swept the floor. He viciously shoved Claudia to one side, unlocked the door and bellowed ferociously at Daisy, 'Murderers are hung!'

Claudia woke with a start and couldn't breathe. She got up, gasping for air. Rushing across the room, she opened the window and filled her lungs with air. She shook her head and wiped tears from her eyes. A sea of fog had gathered outside. It was dense and she couldn't see very much apart from the gas lamps flickering in the street. She heard voices and moved towards the door, listening to familiar mutterings between Arnold and the servants.

'That's it!' she cried. They *had* missed something!

Immediately, she ran out and round to Hugo's room, where she knocked urgently on the door.

'Hugo! Let me in,' pleaded Claudia, rattling the door knob. 'I need to speak to you.'

'What's going on?' Hugo rubbed his eyes and squinted as he opened the door.

'I won't be long,' said Claudia, pushing past him. 'Where's Arnold's fingerprints?'

Hugo's frowned and looked confused. He froze, staring at her for several seconds before he spoke. Claudia guessed that the suggestion that the most important servant in the house would deceive the family was impossible to comprehend.

'Surely you don't think that he's involved in any of this?' He has served my family honourably for years and my father trusts him implicitly.'

'So you didn't get them?'

Hugo shook his head.

'But it can't do any harm to dismiss him from our investigation. It's not fair that we've tested all the other servants' prints but not his.'

'I really don't know, Claudia. And it's late. Can we speak about this again in the morning?'

'But what about Daisy…?'

'It's too late, Claudia. I want to help, but how can we get fingerprints at this time of night? We'd have to wait until Arnold's asleep and sneak into his room. We might as well wait until we can get them tomorrow morning when he's moving around.'

'OK. Goodnight Hugo.' Claudia reluctantly agreed, although she was worried about wasting time. Hugo was right; it would be too dangerous. If Arnold caught them, they'd be in massive trouble with Hugo's parents.

'Good night, Claudia.'

She slipped back to her own room, wondering whether she should try to get Arnold's prints herself. Claudia paced up and down in her room, wrestling with her feelings. She couldn't sleep – she couldn't even sit still. Then she realised she could hear gentle knocking. She tentatively opened the door and peeped around.

'It's only me,' whispered Hugo, holding a hot drink. 'Can I come in?'

'Of course you can.'

Claudia stepped aside. 'I'm sorry if I upset you.'

'Not at all,' Hugo said. 'I have to admit that it didn't enter my head that Arnold would be involved in any of this. But then I thought about it. After you left, I popped downstairs. Fortunately, Arnold was at the kitchen table, reorganising the staff's duties.'

'What did you do?' Claudia asked.

'I told him that I couldn't sleep, so he made me a drink and handed it to me.'

'Quick,' urged Claudia, hurrying across the room, grabbing her bag and taking out the powder. Hugo quickly put the cup on the table near the window. 'There they are,' he said pointing to the fingerprints. Claudia rushed to the table and compared the print to the one that she had found in the dressing room.

'Well?' asked Hugo.

25

DAMNATION ALLEY

Claudia drew back her hand like she was releasing a razor blade.

'What is it?' Hugo shuffled closer.

'It's a match!'

'Arnold is involved?' gasped Hugo.

'He probably planned the whole thing with Jack and Foggy,' said Claudia, remembering the conversation they'd had about jewellery.

Hugo asked quizzically, 'Who are they?'

'Two pirates that I overheard planning a robbery. Remember when we spotted him in the town when he should have been here working? I bet he was meeting them then.'

'Arnold may have stolen some jewellery, but I'm sure he wouldn't have murdered Violet.'

'Maybe you're right, but he's definitely involved with some shady characters,' Claudia took a deep breath, 'and I spotted him scooting down the stairs when I left the dressing room. He's been watching us the whole time.'

Hugo's face was as white as a sheet. 'Arnold has betrayed my family,' he said, pulling the prints towards him. 'He's nothing but a dirty, rotten, scoundrel.'

'You're right,' agreed Claudia, 'and he lied to me, too.'

'What do we do now?' asked Hugo. 'You know

my father will never believe it, and nor will Inspector Squibbs.'

They heard footsteps outside the bedroom, receding down the stairs. Claudia jumped up and looked out of the door. She could see the familiar trails of Arnold's servant's uniform in the hallway. A few seconds later, a distant door slammed shut.

She turned back to Hugo. 'Arnold! He must have heard us talking!'

Hugo squinted out of the window into a fog-filled street. 'Where do you think he's gone?'

'Come on,' said Claudia, making for the door, 'we had better follow him.'

'Are you sure?' asked Hugo, taking her arm. 'Do you really want to get involved in all of this?'

'I have to,' she said, breaking free. This was her chance to clear Daisy's name.

They rushed out of the room, ran down the stairs, grabbed their coats hanging in the hall, and flew out of the front door into the street.

'Which way did he go?' Claudia spun round.

'I have no idea. The fog's too thick to see.'

They heard a scuffle amongst some branches nearby.

'Look!' Hugo pointed to the noise. 'It's Sekora.'

'Did you see which way Arnold went?' asked Claudia, certain that he would understand.

Sekora swivelled his head around and then he sprinted along the road.

'Quick! I think he wants us to follow him.'

'OK,' said Hugo. 'Let's go!'

Claudia and Hugo raced along the narrow streets, chasing Sekora. He scampered through an alleyway that separated the fishmonger's shop from a row of terraced cottages. Then he pounced over a pile of crates and a barrel of ale stacked outside a pub. After several minutes, the glossy black cat stopped outside a butcher's shop.

'Does he want us to wait here?' panted Hugo, slumping against the shop door.

'I think so. But where are we?' whispered Claudia.

Hugo looked up, straining to read the street sign. 'It's Damnation Alley.'

'Hmm… nice name. Where's Sekora gone?' said Claudia, afraid he had carried on without them. Then she looked over the road and spotted him. Sekora was hiding in the door of a shabby old shop with dirty windows and a sign hanging off the wall, saying, 'Percy Pertwee, Pawnbroker'.

'That's it!' exclaimed Hugo. 'Arnold's trying to sell my mother's jewellery.'

'Hugo, you'll have to go and get Squibbs!' pleaded Claudia. 'Then he can catch Arnold red-handed.'

'I can't leave you here.'

Claudia put a firm hand on his shoulder. 'You have to go. Squibbs is more likely to believe you than me. And I need to stay here to keep an eye on what happens.'

Hugo squeezed Claudia's hand. 'Be careful. Go back to the house if it gets too dangerous.'

'Don't worry about me. Just hurry back.'

'I know a short cut to the police station from here,' said Hugo. 'I'll be back as soon as I can.'

As Hugo left, Claudia eyed the dimly lit shop. Sekora had vanished, but behind the grimy windows she could see the shadows of two men, arguing.

She watched for a while, growing more and more frustrated that she couldn't hear what they were saying. *I'm sorry, Hugo, I can't wait here any longer. I've got to see what Arnold's up to.*

She sped across the road, and slipped around the back of the shop. A warped wooden door at the back was ajar. She let herself into the dusty back room of the shop and crouched down, straining to hear the conversation.

'I've told you, that's not enough!' snarled Arnold angrily. 'Foggy said you would give me a good price.'

'Don't be greedy,' sighed Percy. 'Gonna be hard shifting this under-the-counter stuff. Whole town's looking for it. I'm going to have to break it down and send it outta town. That cuts into my profit.'

'I haven't got time to mess around!' demanded Arnold, his voice suddenly high. 'How much for the brooches?'

'Not much sparkle,' complained Percy. Claudia guessed he was holding one up to the light. 'Ya gotta remember I only pay second-hand prices.'

'Don't start that again. They're the best quality diamonds and you know it.'

'Got any gold?' said Percy gruffly. 'That's easier to get rid of.'

'Plenty,' said Arnold, and Claudia heard the tinkling of chains.

Unfortunately, that was also the moment that she sneezed.

26

PERCY PERTWEE PAWNBROKER

Hugo sprinted into the station. He fell against the counter and banged his hand on the bell. He already regretted leaving Claudia outside the shop. What if she did something stupid?

'I NEED TO SPEAK TO INSPECTOR SQUIBBS!' he yelled.

'Master Hugo, what on earth is going on?' asked Constable Horrod, frowning.

'Did I hear my name being called?' Squibbs emerged from the back office, looking red-faced and flustered.

'Listen to me!' Hugo thumped the counter.

'Calm down and explain what's happened,' replied Squibbs, stepping from around the counter towards Hugo.

'Arnold Leech stole my mother's jewellery!'

'Arnold Leech?' repeated Squibbs. 'I don't believe a word of it. He's worked for your father for years, and I've never heard a bad word said against him.'

'He's in Damnation Alley right now, trying to sell it,' shouted Hugo. 'My friend Claudia stayed behind to watch him. Come and see for yourself if you don't believe me!'

'Alright, Master Hugo. I think it's best we do that! Let's go, Horrod,' shouted Squibbs, grabbing his coat.

Hugo dashed out of the station, pointing the way wildly. 'This way!' he shouted, running like the wind, using every short cut he could think of to get there as quickly as possible.

'We're right behind you,' panted Squibbs.

After several minutes, Hugo came to an abrupt halt across the road from the pawnbrokers shop. 'Oh no...' His face went white. He was staring at the empty doorway. 'Where's Claudia? I knew I shouldn't have left her here alone.'

'Don't worry – if she is in trouble, we'll find her,' replied Squibbs, his hand resting on Hugo's shoulder.

Hugo scratched his head and said, 'She has to be here somewhere.'

'Don't worry, she can't be far,' said Squibbs. 'Let's speak to Percy. He may know something.'

Hugo nodded.

They ran across the road. Squibbs lifted his fist and banged on the window. 'Open up!'

Hugo saw Percy shuffle towards the door and release it a fraction. Horrod stepped forward and shoved it wide open, and Percy bounced back and fell against a display cabinet.

Squibbs picked up a diamond bracelet off the counter and Hugo cried, 'That's my mother's!'

'Search the shop, Constable Horrod!' ordered Squibbs.

Hugo and Horrod dashed out through the back.

'W-what ya want?' said Percy, trembling. 'There's no-one here.'

'Claudia!' shouted Hugo. 'Where are you?'

'It's no use denying what's been going on,' said Squibbs impatiently. 'We know all about it. So, where's the girl?'

'She's not out the back!' hollered Horrod, as he returned to the shop with Hugo at his side.

Percy flattened himself against the wall, clutching

his arms and shaking his head.

'You had better tell us quickly,' warned Squibbs, 'or you'll be charged with receiving stolen property.'

'Stolen property,' repeated Percy. 'I'm not a thief!'

'I'm giving you one last chance to tell us the truth,' threatened Squibbs. 'Who was here earlier?'

'Arnold Leech,' gulped Percy. 'He just wanted me to buy some jewellery that was left to him by his mother.'

'What about the girl?' snapped Squibbs.

'I remember now.' Percy scratched his head. 'There was someone hiding out the back who he grabbed. But I had nothing to do with it.'

'Take him down the station for questioning,' ordered Squibbs.

'I've got to go,' muttered Hugo, dashing out of the door.

'Go straight home,' insisted Squibbs. 'We'll look for the girl.'

But Claudia was all Hugo could think about. Arnold might have done anything to her! Hugo ran out and spotted Sekora at the corner.

Crouching down to the cat, he asked, 'Can you help me find Claudia?'

Sekora turned and scampered down an alleyway.

'Keep going!' bellowed Hugo, as he sprinted along the uneven cobbled stones, terrified that Arnold wouldn't hesitate to kill again. They ran through the town, up a steep hill, and towards the edge of the cliff. Hugo had no idea where they were going. He hoped that the cat was really guiding him in the right direction, and not just running away.

A lightning bolt flashed through the sky bringing a storm with it. Hugo struggled against the howling wind and huge hailstones.

'Chillingbone Castle!' Hugo frowned. 'Why would Arnold run to Uncle Septimus, the judge, jury, and executioner? Unless…' Hugo's eyes grew wide 'my uncle has something to do with the crime. If so, the conspiracy must have gone far beyond anything anyone could have imagined. He has the power to do whatever he wants, not even Squibbs would stand in his way.'

Sekora yowled loudly and pawed at the wrought iron gates.

'Claudia had better not come to any harm!' said Hugo under his breath. He hoped that he could find her in time.

27

THE ICE HOUSE

'Come on,' Arnold said, as he dragged Claudia by her arm along the endless corridors of the castle. When they reached an arched door, Arnold stopped suddenly, opened it, and pushed Claudia inside a dark wood-panelled room. She stumbled forward, shuddering at the sight of a giant, stained glass window that was emblazoned with a black vulture.

'What's *she* doing here?' snarled a deep voice.

Claudia turned around, trembling violently and gasped in horror. *Septimus Snail! I don't believe it!*

Snail was sat behind a desk, toying with a large purple gemstone. He met her gaze and gave her a threatening stare that chilled her blood.

'I was at Percy's selling some of the jewellery,' said Arnold angrily, 'and I found her out the back.'

Snail's face flushed deep red and he slammed his fist on the desk. 'Why were you spying on Arnold, little girl?'

'I-I wasn't,' stuttered Claudia.

Arnold took Claudia's arm and pushed her roughly into a chair in front of the desk. She collapsed into it, still shaking.

'Don't lie,' Snail stared at her menacingly, his dark eyes drilling into hers. 'Who put you up to this?'

'Nobody,' faltered Claudia.

Snail held up the gemstone and grinned slyly.

'This purple diamond will make me very wealthy. Do you know why Lucinda hid it in her dress?'

'No idea.' Claudia was relieved to see that the stone had been removed from the claw setting. According to Hugo, that meant it had lost part of its power.

'She knows a lot more than she's letting on,' said Arnold shaking his head. 'I've seen her creeping about the house, searching the mistress's dressing room, and asking nosey questions about Daisy.'

'What were you looking for?' Snail scowled.

Claudia willed herself to stop shaking, but it was impossible.

'I promised I'd help Hugo clear Daisy's name. He knew she didn't do it.'

'I might have guessed my idiot nephew was at the bottom of this,' said Snail.

Snail rested the diamond on a silver inkstand and stood up. He walked around his desk and headed to the far corner of the room where a shallow bronze box with lion's paw feet was sat on the edge of a long table. He took out a brass key from his inside pocket, unlocked it, and lifted out a glass case containing a huge, shiny spider with sharp fangs. He opened the lid, plunged his hand inside and pulled the spider out.

He moved ominously towards Claudia and thrust the spider in her face. 'Meet the deadliest spider in the world. I trained him myself!' He laughed loudly, sending shivers up Claudia's spine. 'He's a real killer!'

Claudia tried to jump out of the chair, but Arnold forced her back down by her shoulders. Claudia was terrified of spiders.

'Tell me everything you know… or I'll let him bite you,' Snail warned, 'and you'll be dead in less than a minute.'

Claudia gasped and her pulse raced.

Snail laid the spider on her arm. 'Start talking!'

Claudia took short panicky breaths and watched it crawl up her arm. Her skin prickled with goose bumps and she shuddered as it scuttled nearer to her neck.

'Hurry up,' Snail shouted, 'or I'll give the spider the order.'

Claudia squeezed her eyes tightly together and held in a scream. She stayed as still as stone, terrified that the spider would bite her.

'Why don't you give her a few moments to cool off,' Arnold suggested. 'Then if she doesn't talk, we can have some fun torturing her in the dungeon.'

Claudia wondered why Arnold had stepped in to save her. Maybe he had heard about the purple diamond and wanted to get any secrets she might know out of her.

'You're right. A slow death is much more interesting to watch,' Snail smirked, as he picked up the spider and returned it to its box. 'Throw her in the ice house. It leads to the dungeons and into the torture chamber.'

Claudia breathed a sigh of relief. Not that the torture chamber sounded much better than a deadly spider bite.

'That's where you'll end up,' Arnold muttered, 'if you don't tell us what you know.'

'I wouldn't take too long, Claudia,' said Snail, clenching his fist. 'If you don't die on the rack, we can always have some fun feeding you to the spirits that occupy the depths of the castle.'

Claudia felt a cold shiver surge through her body with the realisation that there was no escape. Arnold stepped forward, yanked her from the chair, and jostled her towards the door.

'You don't have much time,' Arnold whispered coldly into Claudia's ear. 'Talk... or die.'

'Why would I know anything? I'm not from here. Who would trust me?'

Arnold squeezed her arm as if he'd break it. 'That fool Hugo for one.'

Arnold dragged Claudia across the snowy lawns and towards the ice house. Hailstones hit her in the face and the wind blew through her long wavy hair. Arnold unlocked the door and threw her inside.

'I'll be back shortly,' he bellowed from the other side of the door as he turned the key. 'When I get back you'd better be in the mood to talk.'

'Let me out of here!' cried Claudia, banging the door with both fists and pleading desperately. 'Please let me out of here!'

28

HELL HOUNDS

Claudia looked around, shuddering in the cold. She was trapped inside a dimly lit room stacked with blocks of ice that formed a high dome around her. She tentatively stumbled across the floor and glared through the rusty bars of a large iron gate that was embedded in one wall. Stretched out in front of her was a dank dark tunnel. She could hear the spooky sound of the spirits wailing in the dungeons. With the door locked, she decided that she had to try and find a way out, and this looked like the only other exit from the room. She took a deep breath and gave the gate a tug. It wouldn't budge an inch and she couldn't slide the bar that bolted it shut.

Claudia's heart gave a horrible lurch. *What can I do? Arnold will be back soon with Snail and they'll torture me to death. Come on, Claudia, think.*

Claudia spun round. Her body was shaking and she felt completely helpless. She could kick herself for being so stupid. Not waiting for Hugo and trying to take matters into her own hands had been a big mistake.

As she paced up and down the ice house, tugging at her long curly hair and wondering what to do, her foot hit something hard. She leant down and yanked open the lid of a shabby wooden toolbox. Inside was a collection of old tools and broken bits of machinery. *I wonder if this might work...* She lifted out a short steel rod, hurried back to the gate and quickly jammed it into a hole at the top of the lock. Then she rummaged through the box and found a sprocket wheel that she pushed onto the rod, engaging the lock. She tried the gate again – but it still wouldn't budge.

Claudia scowled and shook her head. She emptied the tools onto the floor and found a handle, slid it into the sprocket, and it turned the bar. Then, astonishingly, the gate clicked open. 'I've done it!' she squealed with delight, pulling out the handle. She dashed through the gate, pushing it shut behind her and threw the handle on the ground.

As she stumbled along the cold, dark, wet passageway her footsteps echoed back at her through the gloom. Her heart thumped and strange notions welled up inside her head. She wondered if she would fall into a pit that would lead her straight to hell.

She paused for a moment; she could smell something stomach-churningly vile. She froze, too scared to go on. Then she imagined Daisy's face, and the thought of her being hung gave Claudia the courage to continue. She sped along the gently descending, winding tunnel towards a blaze of torches.

At last, I'm through! She guessed she was in the deepest part of the castle. Claudia saw dungeons in front of her and heard a strange, howling sound. Hooks and instruments of torture were scattered across the stone floor. Grisly skeletons were tied to vertical racks and were hanging from chains inside the cells. As she crept forward, a mountain of barrels as high as the chamber loomed over her. She craned her neck to look up, and an unpleasant metallic scent filled her nostrils. She slowly lifted a lid from one of the barrels and jumped back in horror. It was filled to the brim with vibrant fresh blood!

Claudia stumbled back, wincing and feeling sick.

Why is Snail collecting blood?

A flash of movement and a growl caught Claudia by surprise. She quickly turned around and froze. Rushing straight towards her were six spirit dogs, teeth bared and drool dripping from their ravenous jaws.

Claudia gasped. The pack of ferocious hounds raced across the floor towards Claudia, baying for her blood. They gathered together, gnashing their razor-sharp teeth and growling loudly.

Claudia made a run for it, towards a different tunnel from the one she'd come in by, but they saw what she was doing, headed her off, blocking the entrance. She skidded to a halt and slowly stepped backwards through some straw lying on the floor. The hounds moved closer, baring their teeth in a vicious snarl. She retreated further to get away from the straw, and grabbed a flaming torch from the wall. She threw it to the floor, lighting the straw and a mighty flame flew up in their faces, forcing them back. While they were distracted, Claudia rushed across the chamber, slipped behind a thick, stone pillar and stayed perfectly still.

Once the flames went out the horde of hounds searched the dungeons, desperately sniffing the ground for human scent. They lifted their heads, howling loudly as one, and then they scampered across the chamber.

As the hounds drew nearer, Claudia took a deep breath, and raced across the dungeon, her heart pounding as fast as her feet, and scrambled up the blood-filled barrels to safety at the top. Using it as a vantage point, she crouched down. The hounds clambered up the barrels. Claudia looked around in terror. If the hell hounds got to the top, she knew that would be the end of her.

She spotted a flat metal bar resting on a barrel. Swiftly grabbing it, she levered it between two barrels, causing an avalanche that crashed down onto the beasts, soaking their bodies in blood. They rolled across the floor, whining and yelping in pain.

That was close. Claudia carefully climbed down the barrel mountain, and made a dash for it down the tunnel she'd been blocked from earlier.

Just a few feet into the tunnel Claudia thought that she heard a noise. She strained her ears, convinced that there was a voice coming from behind her. Stopping abruptly she noticed a heavy oak door. She quickly yanked it open.

29

CLAUDIA'S MIND GETS BLOWN

Claudia's jaw dropped, her eyes transfixed by the horrible sight. Dragging their feet across the floor was a hoard of ragged beings with grey, misty flesh. They had seen her and were closing in, babbling amongst themselves. No noses, no ears, just eerie eyes and enormous open mouths. The strange beings moved closer, bellowing incomprehensible words, seemingly desperate to outdo each other. The babbling din was overwhelming, like the high-pitched squeak of fingernails scraping on slate.

'Get back!' Claudia shouted, clutching her hands over her ears.

But the babbling increased in volume. Claudia's ears burned with the pain of the sound. The creatures puckered their lips. It felt as if they were sucking her brain out of her head. They were inside her thoughts. Claudia's brain bubbled, and she collapsed against the wall, confused and disorientated, hands clasped over her ears in agony. She opened her mouth to speak, but instead let out a horrified shriek. She could see familiar faces flashing before her eyes and then being torn apart, one by one.

'Oh no you don't!' she shouted furiously. 'You're not destroying my memories.'

With great difficulty, Claudia focussed on Daisy to make sure that they didn't wipe her from her brain.

She ignored the stabbing pain in her head, edging her way along the wall. She stumbled back through the door. But she couldn't shut it quickly enough, and the creatures chased after her. They swirled around her, circling, desperate to devour her memories and drive her into delirium.

'I will never forget Daisy!' She knew she had to shatter the sinister sound before her memories melted away, and she was left with an empty head. As if instructed by an instinct, she raised her arm. Suddenly, she felt an intense heat surge through her body. Her muscles tensed and then tingled, and she felt a strange discharge of electricity course through her body. Her eyes widened with surprise. She felt stronger and far more powerful than she had ever felt before.

Instinctively, she visualised herself standing inside a solid stone structure. Then, as if bending to her will, a tower rapidly rose out of the ground, built from the dusty floor. It ignited with a magical, blue glow, turning the dust to glass-like bricks around her so fast that the babbling diminished from her mind.

Whoa! What the…?

She was rooted to the spot, feeling perplexed. She knew it shouldn't have been possible, but somehow some kind of incredible intuition had driven her to create it.

The strange beings scuttled closer. They smashed their withered fists against the tower until their knuckles dripped with blood, mouthing screams that Claudia couldn't hear. She braced herself. The tower began to shake. Bricks cracked and the whole thing started to crash to the ground.

'Help me! Someone, help me!' cried Claudia, terrified that her memories would be gone for good and she would be left with a hollow head.

The creatures each drew a long, rattling breath and more babbling burst from their mouths. They stretched out their withered arms and tried to grab her.

'Get back!' Claudia shouted angrily. She fixed her eyes on the failing tower, summoned her inner power, and focussed all her energy on strengthening its walls once again. The bricks expanded and the tower sprung back up, growing taller and stronger than before.

The bizarre beings pounded on the walls furiously, but this time the bricks were unbreakable.

I can't believe that it's possible! Claudia collapsed against the wall and clasped her aching head in her hands. She thought of Daisy, relieved that her memory was still intact.

Abruptly, the babbling creatures mouths slammed shut. They gathered together and scurried away, like sleepwalkers being led back to their beds. Claudia had defeated them. But how? What she'd done scared her, although she'd do it again if she had to.

The tower dismantled, one brick at a time, disappearing down to a heap of glassy dust. Claudia stared at it, her brain struggling to keep up with the craziness of what had happened. Had she just used magic?

She shook her head, knowing that she needed to keep going, and rushed on through the tunnel and through a stone archway. She had to find a way to get out of here. *Please let there be a way out!*

30

THE ARMY OF LOST AND FOUND SOULS

'Claudia,' echoed a voice in the tunnel, 'where are you?'

'I'm here!' she bellowed back. She couldn't quite believe the voice she heard.

'Thank goodness. You're safe.' Hugo emerged from the darkness, panting and wide-eyed. 'I had to break into here. Squibbs was taking too long.'

'We have to get out of here,' cried Claudia, rubbing her eyes in disbelief. It really was Hugo in front of her.

'What's been happening?' Hugo's voice was laced with worry.

'Arnold and Snail are working together and he has the purple diamond,' Claudia warned, 'and he's threatened to kill me. There's not a moment to lose.'

Hugo's face paled as he wailed. 'Oh, no!' He was physically shaking with anger now. 'I have a terrible feeling that my uncle was involved in Violet's murder and the theft of the purple diamond!'

'I'm sorry,' Claudia blurted, 'but we'd better get going. Now!'

'I didn't want to believe it... but I was suspicious as to why Arnold had brought you here.'

'Which way?' pleaded Claudia, raising her arms in desperation. 'How did you get in? Can we follow that path back out?'

'I'm not sure - I've been wandering around down

here for ages,' admitted Hugo, 'and all the corridors look the same. I have no idea how I managed to find you.'

'Where do you think you're going?' yelled Snail, his face burning red with anger. He had appeared in the passageway.

Arnold leapt in front of Hugo and Claudia, and they skidded to a halt.

'I never thought you'd have the nerve to come here, Hugo,' Snail said. 'I'm actually quite impressed. Didn't think you had it in you.'

'You'll wish you had never been born,' Arnold said with a smirk.

Snail nodded. 'It's unfortunate that I'll have to kill my nephew. Ah, well, never mind.'

Hugo gasped. 'You won't get away with this,' he snapped, waving his fist in Snail's face. 'My father will hunt you down!'

'Forget that, you fool,' blasted Snail, spittle spraying from his mouth. 'This is between us.'

Claudia's body trembled. She glanced around, wondering which way they should run.

'Mark my words,' Snail warned. 'By the end of the night you'll be on your knees begging to tell me everything you know.' He snapped his fingers.

The terrifying sound of tormented souls screamed all at once, desperate to be revived. Claudia pressed her hands to her ears to silence the commotion. The dungeon walls shook, and three tall, broad-shouldered spirits burst through the walls, each dressed for battle with a shield and sword.

Claudia raised her eyebrows and gasped.

'This will teach you to interfere in our business,' said Arnold.

Snail flailed his arms into the air. 'Meet the soldiers from the Army of Lost and Found Souls. I've built the greatest fighting force ever formed.'

'More like cheap minions,' Hugo said, glaring at the soldiers with a determined look on his face.

'Only Dorcas can stop soldiers as strong as these,' whispered Claudia, shaking with fear. 'We need her.'

Snail laughed, his mouth twisting cruelly. 'It'll be fun watching you die!'

'Run for it, Claudia!' Hugo shouted. He lunged forward and shoved Snail out of their way.

Snail fell to the floor, barking at the soldiers. 'Don't let them get away!'

The warriors advanced, swishing their swords in circles above their heads. Hugo and Claudia bolted along a dark tunnel, until they got to a row of arched wooden doors embedded in a stone wall, the soldiers in hot pursuit.

'It's no use,' Hugo tugged the first door. 'It's locked.'

Claudia quickly moved onto the next one, pulling as hard as she could. It didn't budge either.

'Quick,' said Hugo. 'Let's try down here.'

They fled down passageways that led them back the way they'd come. As they ran they looked around, afraid that the army would appear at any minute.

'It's useless,' panted Claudia. 'We're trapped!'

'Don't give up,' Hugo urged. 'We have to keep going.'

In the distance they could hear Snail commanding his troops, ordering them to search the tunnels. 'Keep looking!' he roared. 'They're around here somewhere.'

'We've got to get out,' whispered Claudia.

'Let's try this way,' urged Hugo.

'There they are!' Arnold shouted.

'Wait, what's over there?' Claudia pointed to an archway covered with loose bricks. They surged forward with renewed energy and began pulling vigorously at the loose bricks. As soon as the wall collapsed enough they climbed onto the pile of broken bricks to find that they were close to the outside world. They could see a silvery moon at the end of one final, short tunnel. Claudia's face lit up as she realised this was a way out.

'Keep going,' Hugo coughed and croaked. 'We're nearly out.'

'I knew we could do it!'

But at that moment, the soldiers filled the tunnel.

'We're done for!' Hugo gasped.

31

DEADLY DUEL

Claudia looked down at them, feeling truly terrified.

'What now?'

'You go,' Hugo urged as he jumped off the mountain of rubble to face the soldiers.

'No, I'm not leaving you here alone.'

'Let's see what you're made of,' Snail shouted.

Claudia bristled. 'We're made of stronger stuff than you!'

'Kill them,' said Snail casually.

'Hand him a sword to make the fight fair,' Claudia pleaded.

'It won't help him!' Snail grabbed a sword out of a soldier's hand and threw it to Hugo.

'Run, Hugo!' begged Claudia.

Hugo shook his head. 'It's too late.'

Claudia could only watch from the top of the pile of bricks. The soldier whipped his razor-sharp sword through the air. Hugo dodged the swirling blade and jumped himself behind a pillar. The soldier rushed forward, but Hugo raised his sword to stop his attacker. Their weapons clashed high in the air, and they stood face to face. Hugo pushed the soldier away and sliced the tip of his weapon around so fast it struck his shoulder. The soldier retaliated by driving his sword so tight against Hugo's throat that a trickle of blood ran down his neck.

'Stop!' Claudia screamed at the top of her voice. At the same time she climbed down the pile of bricks.

'Dying is a messy business,' Snail hissed with a grin.

'Get out of here!' Hugo shouted at Claudia. 'Save Daisy! Tell the others about Uncle Septimus.'

Snail raised his arm to give the order. 'Don't you want to watch him die?'

'Wait!' Claudia pleaded, her lips trembling. 'Don't harm him.'

'Ignore her,' Snail yelled. 'Hugo will soon be joining the soldiers from hell.'

'Leave him alone!' Claudia burst out, focusing on her inner strength, desperately trying to summon something that would stop Snail's soldier slitting Hugo's throat.

'Finish him!' Snail ordered.

'No!' Claudia fixed her eyes on Hugo.

Hugo pushed the soldier away with a foot and made a run for it.

'Get him!' bellowed Snail. The soldier charged after him.

Claudia checked her surroundings, and saw a pile of torture tools strewn across the floor, outside a cell. She ran across the chamber, feeling a new strength surge through her. Kneeling down, she grabbed an armful of what appeared to be torture implements and without knowing what she was doing, she started to put them together.

As she pushed a pillywink into a spiked collar, she realised that she was building a dog. All at once, it was like the blueprint was laid out in front of her. She was building it with no problem at all. Her hands moved feverishly, the tools took over and started to lock together, coiling and spinning over one another, fuelled by her mysterious force. In the briefest of time a mechanical dog stood before her. Her hands felt like they were on fire, but in a good way. Splaying her fingers, she held her palms above the mechanical beast and concentrated hard.

The giant mechanical dog, with its rotating head and spring-loaded legs, reared up in front of her. Its metal body was powered by cylindrical gears, interlocking cogs, levers and chains, and it towered over her.

Claudia jumped up, amazed by what she had done. She felt the hairs stand up on the back of her neck. She looked at the dog, confused, surprised, and a little proud of her actions, but with no idea where her power came from. She had breathed life into a machine!

The dog stamped his feet, sending a loud, high-pitched whirring sound off the walls with great bouts of steam hissing out of its nostrils.

'That was amazing!' Hugo gasped, managing to push away his attacker. 'What did you do?'

There was no time to explain. Soldiers were gathering around the dog, swinging their swords at it. The dog took a step back, flashing its sharp fangs. Streams of fire flew from the metal mouth, vaporising the soldier's souls. One by one, they disintegrated into clouds of black dust.

Hugo's eyes widened.

'There's plenty more where they came from!' Snail shouted, snapping his fingers.

A new soldier advanced through the wall, holding a club with spiked iron balls attached by thin chains. When Snail gave the order to attack, the soldier circled the flail in the air. The mechanical dog hummed and hissed and charged across the stone floor at high speed, and easily flattened the soldier that stood in its way. The immediate danger seemed to have passed, but Claudia was still wary.

'Claudia! There's someone coming!' Hugo called.

'Septimus!' cried a voice. 'Septimus, where are you?'

'What is it, Agatha?' Snail shouted.

Help had arrived. *I'd better not let anyone else see what I've just made!* Claudia motioned to her creation, and the eyes flashed, and it barked loudly as it made its way towards her, obediently lowering its head. She smiled and nodded, clicked her fingers and shut it down. Instantly, the eyes closed, mouth snapped shut, and it started to dismantle. Components rolled across the floor, disappearing into the dimly lit dungeon.

'Thanks,' Claudia muttered to the memory of her dog, and raced over to Hugo.

'A disturbance was reported to the police station,' said Lady Agatha, hurrying towards her husband. Inspector Squibbs and Constable Horrod followed closely behind her. Squibbs stepped forward, glaring around the gloom. 'What's been happening?'

'Thank goodness you're here.' Snail cleared his throat and pulled something out of his pocket. 'I've retrieved the purple diamond. Arnold Leech here, stole it and then had the audacity to try and sell it to me!'

'Lying, cheating, fool!' Arnold's face screwed up in anger and disbelief. 'You promised to protect me…'

'And he murdered Violet!' said Snail, handing the sparkling stone to Squibbs.

Arnold slowly stepped back towards the shadows, and then he ran off.

'Grab him!' Squibbs bellowed.

Horrod chased Arnold across the dungeon and they disappeared down a dark passage.

Shouts echoed off the walls and Horrod yelled loudly. 'Got him, sir! I'll take him straight to the station.'

'I knew he wouldn't get far,' muttered Squibbs.

Hugo and Claudia stepped out from the shadows.

'What are you two doing here?' Lady Agatha

asked Hugo and Claudia.

'They followed Arnold here,' Snail said hastily.

Squibbs shook his head. 'I thought I told you to go straight home, Hugo.'

'Snail was working with Leech!' blurted out Claudia.

'She's right,' said Hugo.

Claudia gave Agatha an anxious look.

'They planned the whole thing together.'

'You've misunderstood, my dear Claudia,' Snail placed his hand firmly on Squibbs's shoulder. 'I only pretended to help Arnold so that I could solve the murder and retrieve the diamond.'

'What are you saying, Claudia?' Lady Agatha spoke in a stern voice. 'My husband would never steal my sister's diamond!'

'Absolutely.' Snail feigned offence. 'Arnold came here tonight to sell me the stone. I knew it was Lucinda's, so I went along with his plan for the sake of the family. I was about to bring him to you, Squibbs.'

The policeman nodded his head respectfully. 'Regardless, I'll need to take a short statement.'

'Of course, Inspector. Anything I can do to help put Arnold behind bars.' Snail turned to his wife. 'You go back to the house, Agatha. I'll be up shortly.'

'Alright, Septimus.' Lady Agatha headed towards a door.

'Let's get out of here. I'm exhausted.' Claudia stumbled forward. 'Will Daisy be released tomorrow, Inspector Squibbs?'

'Of course,' he replied. 'I'll deal with the paperwork as soon as I return to the station.'

'Arnold told me this evening,' explained Snail 'that he planned the whole thing with two ruffians called Foggy and Jack, a couple of pirates who often frequent the Dog and Duck. Inspector Squibbs, you might want to investigate there next.'

'Yes indeed,' Squibbs nodded his head. 'I thought Arnold couldn't have been working alone.'

'After you, Inspector.'

'Most kind,' said Squibbs, marching ahead.

Snail suddenly turned around to Hugo and Claudia, and he gave them a sinister grin, whispering, 'Come along, you two. It's cold down here.'

Claudia shivered, as though a poison raced through her veins. She knew that Snail was on to her and she was afraid of what he might do.

'We're coming,' Hugo glanced at Claudia, shaking his head in disbelief at how Snail had got out of the situation. She smiled knowingly back at him. Claudia burned with fury inside. The precious jewel had been recovered, and her main goal of Daisy being freed had succeeded... but Hugo's family had been betrayed and Snail had got off scot free.

'Huh... law and order,' Hugo muttered under his breath as they trailed out of the dungeon. 'It's all an act! He was prepared to watch me and you die. And he'd have hung Daisy tomorrow if we hadn't got to him first.'

'There has to be a way to make him pay for what he's done,' Claudia said with determination.

'You're right,' replied Hugo. 'But his story was very convincing, and I think Squibbs is too afraid of him.'

Claudia's eyes flashed with anger. 'I'm staying in Pencliff until Daisy is definitely released.'

32

SECRET BLOODLINE

Claudia flopped onto the bed, covered herself with a warm blanket, blew out the candle next to the bed, and quickly fell asleep. She slept peacefully, without being woken by bad dreams. The following morning, she woke, for the first time in a while feeling refreshed, if still a little tired. She stretched out her arms, jumped out of bed, and pulled on her dress.

KNOCK! KNOCK!

Claudia turned to the door and gulped. 'Who is it?'

'It's only me,' said Hugo entering the room. 'How are you feeling?'

'A lot better, but very confused.'

Hugo sat on the end of the bed.

'We're lucky to be alive,' said Claudia.

Hugo groaned. 'Arnold double-crossed my family and was working for Uncle Septimus.'

'It's terrible, but what can you do? Hugo... I need to know something. How was I able to fight Snail's spirits?' asked Claudia, shaking her head with confusion. 'And how did I conjure up a mechanical dog while we're on the subject?'

'You have the gift! I don't know about the mechanical dog though. I've never seen someone building something like that. But the rest is magic.' Hugo's eyes flashed with excitement. 'It's an inner strength that you will have to learn to develop.'

'But how?' A tingle of excitement flooded through Claudia. She wasn't quite sure how she felt about knowing she had magical powers.

Hugo took a deep breath and suggested, 'Maybe Dorcas can help you.'

It's time to tell Hugo the truth.

'I know I should have told you before, but Jasper is my great-grandfather. I travelled here from the future in a grandfather clock that Jasper built.'

Hugo's eyes bulged. 'You… you're kidding?'

Claudia stifled a laugh, thinking that he was beginning to sound like her. 'It's true, and when I'm away from home, time stands still.'

'I wonder why Dorcas didn't tell me,' Hugo said in amazement.

'Err… maybe Jasper doesn't want anyone to know about me. Let's keep this between us for the moment please, Hugo.'

'Of course. Now it all makes sense,' Hugo paused for a moment. 'Your ancestors are part of a secret bloodline and you're part of it too, even though you're only distantly related. Whatever blood pumps through your veins, also pumps through Jasper, Dorcas and Snail.'

Claudia's eyes widened. 'How many of us are there?'

'I don't know,' Hugo sighed. 'Unfortunately, I don't have the gift, since I'm not related by blood to my uncle. He just married my Aunt Agatha.'

'What if I just want to be ordinary again?'

She wasn't sure she could embrace her gift.

'You can't ignore who you are,' said Hugo, determination flashing in his eyes. 'You're special.'

'It's so strange that I didn't know I had this special power.' Claudia looked uncertainly at Hugo.

'Something deep inside of you,' Hugo said calmly,

'must have awakened your inborn ability.'

Claudia thought that part of it sounded exciting, part of it was terrifying.

'Let's get something to eat,' Hugo said, leaping off the bed and heading for the door.

Claudia picked up her bag and swung it over her shoulder. As they headed along the landing, Claudia spotted a servant coming out of a bedroom carrying a breakfast tray with a newspaper tucked under the plate.

'Excuse me, is that today's paper?' she asked, desperate for some news of Daisy. 'Could I have quick look?'

'Of course,' replied the servant. 'Lady Puckett has finished with it.'

Claudia took the newspaper, unfolded it, and read out the front page headline.

'DAISY RATCHET NOT GUILTY!'

We did it!

'Look at this, Hugo,' said Claudia, holding it up and smiling triumphantly. 'I bet Snail is furious.'

'That's wonderful news,' Hugo replied, as they descended the stairs and hurried to the dining room.

'It's all thanks to you!'

'No, Hugo, we did it together.'

'Good morning,' said the butler as they entered the room. 'Can I get you anything?'

Hugo pulled out a chair politely for Claudia.

'We'll just help ourselves, thank you, Alfred.'

At the centre of the table was a bowl of pale pink roses, surrounded by silver dishes with fresh fruit, bacon, sausages, eggs, toast, butter, and a pot of tea.

Claudia helped herself to some ruby red grapes. 'Is Daisy coming back to work? I'd love to meet her.'

'Apparently not.' Hugo shook his head. 'She collected her things early this morning. She told my father that she needed a fresh start, so she accepted a position at Chillingbone Castle because her husband was working there.'

'Chillingbone Castle…?' repeated Claudia.

Hugo shook his head. 'Daisy has no idea what a treacherous, two-faced villain Snail is.'

Claudia couldn't stop her eyes filling with tears. She'd hoped that she could have explained to Daisy who she was. Maybe it wasn't the right time.

'Why the sad face?' asked Hugo.

Claudia thought quickly. 'It's time to say goodbye. I have to go home.'

'Surely you don't need to go just yet?' Hugo sighed with obvious disappointment. 'There's so much more to do. Snail's still free.'

'I promise to come back soon.' Claudia realised that her adventure was only just beginning. 'But I need to go back to my family.' She wanted to find out what had really happened to Daisy, now she hadn't been hanged. *How did this change the history of Pencliff?*

'I understand,' Hugo said, wiping his mouth in his napkin as he got to his feet. 'In the meantime, I'll speak to Dorcas and tell her about your gift.'

As they left the dining room together, Claudia spotted Sekora in the hallway. He scampered towards her, his pink eyes sparkling.

'Don't stay away too long, Claudia.' Hugo's voice trembled as he spoke. 'We've only just become friends.'

Claudia blinked, holding back tears. She'd grown to like Hugo a lot. He was a better friend than anyone she knew back home. But all she could say was, 'Watch out for Snail.'

'He needs to watch out for me!'

Claudia laughed.

'Have a safe journey home,' he said.

'I will.' Claudia picked up Sekora and stroked his head. As she walked towards the grandfather clock and opened the door, she paused for a moment. She felt one of her fingers tingle. *Hmm.* A crescent-shaped mark had appeared on the tip of her index finger, just like the one on Sekora's head. *What's this?* Claudia stared at her finger in disbelief. She wondered if it was some strange gift from Sekora… or maybe it had something to do with Jasper… She wasn't sure where it came from, or what it meant. *I hope my parents don't spot it!* She knew she would have to forget about her gift while she was at home. She didn't want her parents asking questions.

Sekora purred loudly and licked her hand.

'Let's go home,' Claudia said to the cat. She hopped inside, slumped against the wall and held on tight as the wild wind turned and swirled the clock. When the clock stopped, she hurried through the open door.

This has been one crazy adventure. Snail may have got away with it, but I did save Daisy from the gallows. I changed the past!

Back in her bedroom, Claudia climbed into bed, still feeling tired despite the sleep she'd got at Hugo's house. The doll's house started to sink, as did her mood. She was already missing Pencliff. She slid into a light sleep.

Snail was stepping inside the clock, then he was running down the long hallway. He entered her bedroom…

A second later, her eyes popped open. She heard a loud rustling noise of footsteps getting closer, and was aware that the curtains were twitching.

'Who's there?' she called.

She jumped out of bed, and peered out of the window nervously. She glanced around, afraid that he'd come after her… but realised that it was only the wind whistling through the trees.

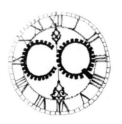

33

THE GRAVES

By the time New Year's Day arrived, Claudia's energy had increased and she was feeling more like her old self. She was tempted to return to Pencliff, but decided not to yet. She got dressed and then gazed out of the window. The snow had stopped falling and the puffins had disappeared. *Why have they suddenly vanished? Did Jasper send the puffins to deliver his letter? Or was it just a coincidence?* Claudia quickly lifted up the mattress and gasped. The letter had disappeared too!

'Happy New Year, Claudia.' Her father opened her bedroom door. 'The taxi will be here in about thirty minutes. Are you all set to go to London?'

'Dad, I've changed my mind. I don't want to go.' Claudia looked at him, pleading with her eyes. 'Can we go to Pencliff instead, to see the family's graves? You promised we could do that too, and I've got that family tree project to complete for school.'

'Alright.' Her father raised an eyebrow. 'I suppose it would be a nice thing to do.'

'Can you check with Mum? I'll be down in a mo.'

'Alright,' her father repeated, and left.

'I won't be too long, Sekora.' Claudia tucked him under her arm and descended the stairs.

'There's something I've got to see. Promise me you'll stay here this time.'

Sekora meowed as if answering in confirmation.

Claudia walked into the kitchen. 'You don't mind going to Pencliff, do you, Mum?'

'Not at all,' her mother said, taking Sekora from Claudia's arms. 'I expect there are plenty of shops there too! I need a long dress for next month's Law Society ball at the city hall.'

Claudia bit her lip. She imagined Lady Lucinda in the beautiful lavender gown she wore to the party and she knew her mother would have loved it.

'I've left some milk in the kitchen for him,' her mother nodded at the silky black cat.

They jumped into the taxi and it sped away, heading towards the train station.

'It's been a really mild winter,' said Claudia's mum. 'Only a few sprinklings of snow.'

'You're right, we've been very lucky,' her father agreed, staring at the bright blue sky. 'It's been the mildest winter I can remember.'

Claudia was surprised. Then she realised that it wasn't only the letter that had disappeared. So had the severe snow and the puffins.

After the train journey and another taxi ride, they were dropped off at a quaint little church in Pencliff. Claudia surged ahead of her parents. Eager to quench her curiosity, she dashed through the wrought iron gate and into a graveyard dotted with gravestones. She was desperate to see her family's graves, although she realised how weird that sounded. At least her parents had believed her story about a family tree project.

'Where are they?' Claudia wandered aimlessly between headstones choked with weeds. 'I can't see them anywhere!'

'Try down there,' her father shouted, waving a finger in the opposite direction.

Claudia turned on her heels and followed a narrow winding pathway lined with violet flowers. At the end of the trail was a circular stone clock. *This had to be it!* She read the engravings and her heart leapt: *Daisy and Jasper Ratchet.* She broke into a beaming smile, delighted that they were reunited. Daisy was no longer buried within the prison walls. Claudia really had changed the past!

'Here they are. It says they died peacefully on the same day.'

'What an unusual design,' her mother said.

'The clock shows the hour of their death,' said Claudia. The hands were set to midnight.

'They had a wonderful life,' her father said with a broad smile, 'a happy marriage, and a successful business.'

Claudia's eyes widened in utter bewilderment. She knew immediately that the gift she'd inherited was indeed powerful. She had not only changed the past, but also her father's feelings towards his ancestors. He'd never spoken about his family when they had been disowned, but now he was proud of them.

Her father nodded. 'I'm glad we came here today.'

Claudia knelt down to clear some dirt that was covering part of the inscription. 'Life is an adventure to be treasured,' she read aloud.

'Look,' said her father, stepping aside and pointing. 'My father is buried right next to his parents.'

'I wish I had met them,' Claudia said sadly.

'I know,' her father put his hand on her shoulder, 'but I'm sure they wouldn't want us to be sad.'

'Are you ready to leave?' asked her mother, wiping tears from her eyes.

Claudia nodded and the three of them headed down the pathway and through the gate. The wind swept wildly through Claudia's hair and it reminded her of the cool sea breeze in Pencliff.

'This way,' her father said. 'Let's visit Jasper's shop.'

'Great idea!' Claudia said excitedly.

34

STATUE WITH A SECRET

As Claudia followed her parents, something caught her eye. She crossed to a cobbled square to admire a beautiful statue of a girl with long wavy hair. The girl was holding a crystal.

'Isn't she lovely?' A woman wearing a plush purple coat had stopped and said to her, 'Jasper Ratchet gifted her to the city.'

Claudia's pulse raced and she was dumbstruck. *Why is she holding a crystal?*

'Hurry up, Claudia,' shouted her father.

'I'm coming!' Claudia felt her face redden. She walked around the statute. Then, she caught sight of the inscription on the back of the stone plinth. 'Use your gift to overcome evil.' She gasped. *That's a message for me! Jasper's telling me to return to Pencliff!*

'Jasper dedicated it to the town,' the lady told Claudia. 'My grandmother knew him well. He always told her that he hoped the statue would inspire young people to use their gifts and follow their dreams.'

Claudia smiled. Jasper had not only honoured her in a very special way, but he had also left her a very important message. Obviously it couldn't have been a statue actually of Claudia, but it was all she needed to see.

'Goodbye,' said the lady as she crossed the road.

Claudia quickened her pace. She followed her

father and mother to the end of the road and towards a street with a row of charming shops with bright rainbow-coloured canopies.

'There it is!' He suddenly stopped to admire the shop. 'Isn't it wonderful!' His face assumed a proud expression as he read the sign: *Ratchet's Exquisitely Designed Clocks*.

Claudia's heart swirled with happiness. She couldn't believe her father's positive reaction absence of any sense of shame he had felt. Above the door was a picture of a mythological goddess with flaming red hair holding a striking moon dial. The figure looked exactly like Dorcas.

'It's certainly a shop from the past,' her mother observed.

'Let's take a look inside.' Her father opened the door for them all to enter.

Claudia paused to read the grand gold lettering on the window, *Services Supplied to the Sovereign*.

'How amazing,' her mother muttered under her breath.

Claudia stepped inside and was immediately mesmerised by the number of clocks that filled the shop. They were every shape and size and looked like the most complicated devices she had ever seen. Not that Claudia was an expert on clocks! But still... At that moment, they struck the half hour. Tiny doors suddenly burst open. Soldiers marched out of the clocks, pointing their swords, and mechanical puffins peeped out of the windows, squawking at the top of their voices.

A tall, thin man, with a receding hairline and a tiny moustache, appeared behind the counter. 'Hello. What can I do for you?'

Claudia stepped forward. 'Hi there. My name's Claudia Quash. My great-grandfather, Jasper Ratchet, used to own this shop.'

'He did indeed. He was a genius and a master horologist. I inherited the shop from my father who was Jasper's business partner. My name is Fred, by the way.'

'Are all these clocks Jasper's designs?' asked Claudia, looking around again.

'Absolutely. Jasper was one of the greatest watchmakers of his generation and an expert at breathing new life into old pieces. He wanted people to enjoy his clocks, and he felt that their life would end if they went to a museum.'

'Hmm, breathing new life…' Claudia mumbled, thinking of her encounter with the mechanical dog she had created.

Her mother stared at a clock on the wall. 'I never realised that he was so successful.'

'How long did Jasper live here for?' asked Claudia.

'All his life. Everyone in the town loved him. After he died the mayor commissioned Pencliff's clock tower to be built on the promenade as a tribute to him. It has the largest face in the world and it is used by ships to help them find their way.'

'It's a moon dial,' muttered Claudia.

'That's right,' said Fred.

The door opened, interrupting their conversation, and a couple entered the shop, puffing and panting. They were carrying a long case clock with a brass dial.

'We've inherited a clock, but it doesn't seem to work,' said the plump man, with a deep voice. 'Would you mind taking a look at it?'

Fred walked towards them. 'Certainly, sir, bring it through to the workshop.'

'We'd better get going.' Claudia's father said to her. 'We can come back again soon.'

'OK,' she agreed. She headed for the door, shouting 'Goodbye!' to Fred.

He waved and smiled. 'It was nice to meet you,

Claudia Quash. Call again any time.'

As Claudia stepped into the street, she stopped for a moment to digest what had just happened. She had so many questions. Jasper hadn't moved to London. *Does that mean* Splints *doesn't exist now? Changing history was a confusing thing!*

She knew she had to return to Pencliff and develop her gift, especially after seeing Jasper's message on the statue. But right now it was time to celebrate the New Year.

'Let's go to London!' her mother suggested. 'They have a wonderful parade today, with street performers and marching bands.'

Her father smiled. 'What a good idea! But not before we take a quick look at Jasper's clock tower.'

Claudia nodded, with a new spring in her step. She wondered what the New Year might bring. She thought about Hugo, and Pencliff, and Snail. Then she wondered what Snail might do to her if she returned to the town. *At least next time I can be a lot more prepared.*

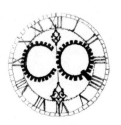

EPILOGUE
CHILLINGBONE CASTLE

Snail escorted Inspector Squibbs out of the castle and promised to provide a written statement first thing in the morning. Slamming the door, he gritted his teeth in silent fury. He stomped across the baronial hall, into his office, and slumped angrily into the chair behind his desk.

'What an almighty mess,' he said, thumping his fist repeatedly on the desk. 'I will not stand for anyone meddling in my business! Those irritating children have cost me a lot of money.'

Snail got up and poured himself a stiff whiskey from his drinks cabinet. He downed it fast and smashed the glass into the fireplace. 'Hugo and Claudia are going to pay heavily for losing me the purple diamond.'

He grabbed his black coat, buttoned it up to his chin, hurried out of his office, and descended the steep steps to the dungeons. Striding through the long, cold corridors, his face burning with anger, Snail made his way through the maze of passageways to a rusty door. He slipped a key into the lock, turned it, and it clanged inwards on creaky hinges. Taking a breath, he stepped inside a high-ceilinged cell, illuminated by wall-mounted oil lamps that cast irregular shadows onto the flagstone floor.

Jasper Ratchet was sitting in the far corner of the

dingy room at the end of a long bench. He was a small man with deep blue eyes and grey streaked hair slicked back behind his ears. He was busy working away, banging sheet metal. At the other end of the bench was a pile of wheels, springs, cogs, and tubes. Behind him, resting up against the wall was an oddly shaped, circular machine that hummed softly.

'You'd better come clean and tell me what's been going on?' Snail's angry voice resonated off the walls. 'Arnold told me that you were seen feeding puffins through that contraption of yours.'

'I was just testing out my new rejuvenation machine,' Jasper explained calmly. 'I sent hundreds of the older birds through it hoping that they would return as baby pufflings - but it didn't work.'

'What happened to them?'

'Err… it sent them to an empty void I think,' Jasper hesitated. 'Anyway what does it matter where they went – the machine doesn't work properly, and I'm going to dismantle it when I have time.'

'You'd better not be lying to me,' Snail slammed his fist down on the bench. 'I've been made a fool of and I won't allow it to happen again.'

Jasper gulped.

'Do you or Daisy know anything about a girl called Claudia, or where she's from?' Snail snapped. 'She's a friend of Hugo's and she's staying with him.'

'Why do you ask?' said Jasper.

'She must be part of the secret bloodline,' Snail said, thoughtfully, pacing up and down. 'She conjured up a mechanical dog that destroyed some of my soldiers.'

Jasper's expression changed. The annoyance passed out of it and, for a moment, his eyes brightened. 'We always knew that there were more of us.'

'I'll make sure that Hugo and Claudia pay for

poking their noses into my business,' Snail warned.

'Forget them. They're only children,' blurted out Jasper. 'Remember, no-one can match your power.'

'You're right, I don't have to rely on machinery like you, or stupid symbols like Dorcas.' Snail rubbed his chin and smiled. 'I'm building the greatest army ever formed and they will allow me to take over the whole country.'

'Building an army is going to take me some time,' Jasper said. 'I've never done this before.'

Snail wandered around the bench, squeezed Jasper's thin shoulder harshly, and bent down to whisper in his ear. 'Daisy is working at the castle now as a maid for Lady Agatha. I'm sure that you wouldn't want anything to happen to her.'

Jasper shook his head and sighed. 'Of course not.'

Snail released his shoulder, picked up a small spring, and spun it between his fingers. 'Well you'd better get on with it. Daisy was lucky to escape the gallows, but her luck could run out.'

'Let me show you something,' Jasper leaned underneath the bench and lifted out a mechanical head. 'I just need to fix it to the body.'

'When they're finished, these machines will have real souls.' Snail said, eyes flashing with blazing fire. 'The most sinister souls in the graveyard.'

'What will we use to keep them alive?'

'I've got barrels of blood, stored in the dungeons.' Snail slicked back his hair and smirked. 'The soldiers will be given the elixir of life…' he scoffed with an ugly laugh. 'The gift of immortality!'

Jasper rolled his eyes. 'If you say so, Septimus.'

'I'll be back tomorrow with some blood. Have it ready by then.' Snail stomped out and the door clanged shut.

Jasper got up and threw the mechanical head on the bench. 'The people of Pencliff will never forgive me for this.' He wandered across the dingy cell and gazed out of the room's narrow window, overlooking the edge of the cliff. The sea raged and the waves crashed against the rocks.

Contemplating his desperate situation, Jasper worried about the power his inventions were giving Snail. He had never meant for it to go this far but, with his wife in danger, he had no other choice but to co-operate. *Oh my! What have I created?*